THE PRINCESS
and the
PROSPECT

Aces High MC - Charleston Book 3

CHRISTINE
MICHELLE

CHRISTINE MICHELLE

COPYRIGHT

NOTE FROM AUTHOR

I don't like doing this, because I honestly don't think books should have to come with warnings. I am relenting in this case, because I know the subject matter is one that many people don't want to read. So in an effort to help out my readers here is your
TRIGGER WARNING!

This book, especially the beginning, may be difficult for some people to read. It was difficult to write because if I were Anna I would have done things so differently. I'm not Anna though, and both she and Tiger Lily represent another view point. I hope that despite people's triggers for certain scenarios that you will read it anyway, because it's the only way to get to the end of the big picture by book five. Just know that I understand the reluctance, I feel your pain, but every character I write cannot be a representation of myself or my personal ideals and choices. Some have to be there to represent people who have made entirely different decisions in their lives. They made them for reasons I'm not privy to, and that I cannot judge because I wasn't walking in their shoes when they were faced with those choices. All of this build up has been to warn you – there is cheating in this book. For the first time ever, I'm writing about cheating that involves the main characters. Granted, the situation may make it seem like a gray area for some, but I'm going to call a spade a spade on this. If you simply can't tolerate reading it, then bail out now. If you can hang in there for a little bit, I promise things work out in the end.

ONE MORE THING

I also want to issue a sincere thank you to everyone who read The Other Princess and were still able to dive head first into the story of A Love So Hard and the man I made you hate in book one. I am a huge fan of writing realism into fiction and exploring the things that make people behave badly or react a certain way. Often times we're quick to judge other people's situations from the comfort of our seats, or when we're looking from the outside in, but when you don't have the full picture it makes things difficult to understand. My goal, other than to entertain, is to make people think. The things we see on the surface of other people's daily lives have deeper roots. Those roots – while you may have never experienced them yourself – affect the choices that people make and the roads they take in their lives. I wish you all the smoothest path to happiness, but I'm wise enough to know that's not possible for everyone. These books are for the people who jumped those hurdles, hit those bumps, and picked themselves up anyway. Even if they managed to mess it up a little more on their journey to smooth sailing. They're also for the people who have been lucky enough never to have to endure the harsher side of life – because for them this is truly fiction.

Thank you again for taking a chance on a new (to you) author, or a new book, and for sticking it out with me this long! Your encouraging messages have meant so much to me! You've also enabled me to teach my children a wonderful lesson in going after your dreams, and not giving up! They have seen me work hard, cry frustrated tears, move past disappointments, and celebrate successes. To me, that is the greatest gift I could give them. Through my own journey to reach my goals they've seen persistence is key, and giving up isn't an option. You have helped me give that to them.
Thank you so much!

Xoxo,
Christine Michelle

CONTENTS

* Prologue   9

1 Shotguns and Wedding Bells   12

2 Honeymoon Hell   29

3 Waking to Nightmares   42

4 Repeating the Past   49

5 Mistakes   62

6 Apologies   73

7 Hiding   89

8 Working It   102

.9 Discoveries   117

10 Dear Diary   131

11 Decked   161

12 Fresh   181

13 It's A Date   188

THE PRINCESS *and the* PROSPECT

14	A Heartbeat	219
15	Rattled	231
16	Settled	240
17	Picture Perfect	249
18	Time's Up	258
**	Epilogue	268
***	Acknowledgments	273
****	JDRF	278
	About the Author	279

MORE MC BOOKS

S.H.E. Series

Angel-Girl

JoJo

Aces High – Dakotas Series

Dancing With Danger

Whiskey Tango Foxtrot

Aces High – Cedar Falls Series

Redemption Weather

Proven

Smoke and the Flame

Aces High – Charleston Series

The Other Princess

A Love So Hard

The Princess and the Prospect

*

PROLOGUE

Age 14

ear Diary,

I can't wait until I can get married and move out of this nuthouse my family calls a home. My mom is being weird all the time. My sister is so emo I honestly don't want to be around her, and my brother – who used to be *her* best friend – isn't around much either. He probably came to the same conclusion about Ever. She's just unhappy, and I don't know why. Daddy gets us anything we want. I know when I ask, he's right there to get me whatever I ask for. Only, he has been riding out to the clubhouse more these days for some reason so I haven't actually been able to ask for things. Not that I was spoiled and took advantage, but Daddy lived to make me happy. I'm sure it was the same for both Toby and Ever too.

Can you see why I want to just get married and move out though? I don't want to know what makes Ever sad, why Toby stays gone all the time, or why Daddy doesn't come home all that much anymore. None of those things are bound to make me happy, and all I want is to be happy, write my stories, and raise my babies with a man who loves me more than anything in the world. That's not too much to ask, is it? It's my dream, and I plan to make it come true.

I mean that too. Everything is all planned out in my head and in my little memory books. I'm going to meet the man of my dreams just before I graduate high school, so I don't have to rush off to college or something else that will waste my time. We're going to start our family while we're young so we can have plenty of energy for those babies and still get to enjoy our lives once they're out of the house. It's my life plan. My wedding is going to be spectacular too.

I already have my dress picked out. It's going to be an amazing ivory gown with tons of lace, and a train so long it trails down half the length of the church aisle. My bridesmaids will be wearing peach and cream floor length dresses and the same color ribbons will be tied to the backs of all the pews in the church. My bouquet will be created using peach Dahlias and white garden roses. It will be tied together in ivory and peach satin ribbon too. My makeup will be done in light tones to compliment the colors as well. My handsome husband would have a peach Dahlia pinned to the lapel of his tux, only he'd tell me that the flowers paled in their beauty when compared to me. We would dance the night away under the stars of a beautiful spring night – because we'd melt in the summertime here in Charleston even when the sun went down – and then he would whisk me away to our honeymoon where our first born would be conceived.

Are you swooning yet? I know I am. My dream is lush, and I don't plan on settling for anything less.

Chapter 1

SHOTGUNS & WEDDING BELLS

Not once in my entire life did I ever think about what my wedding day would look like. Then again, I never expected to be the groom in a goddamn shotgun wedding before either; yet that was exactly where I found myself.

The only saving grace I had in my favor was that this was the result of her lies. Her dubious plan to nab herself a baby daddy and husband worked beautifully, but since she got her way by handing me a load of shit as a background story, lying about her age, who she was, and probably everything else; I wasn't about to give in on the other demands her family had tried to make. They wanted their little girl to have the sweet wedding she used to write about in her journals. Fuck that. There was nothing sweet about being forced to marry the little brat. No, all she was getting from me was a trip to the Justice of the Peace at the courthouse, some nicer than usual denim jeans, and a button up shirt. I couldn't wear my kutte into the courthouse or else I'd be donning that too. Though, truth be told, that kutte and me were not on friendly terms right now either. If it had been anyone else's daughter, I could have just slipped the lying bitch some child support, or taken the kid from her once it was born. Nope, I'm not that lucky. Instead, her daddy, Double-D, was the Vice President of Aces High Motorcycle Club. Yeah, the very some club I had spent the last year prospecting for. I'd finally become a member, just in time to find out I was also going to be a daddy and the mom had already turned out to be a lying bitch.

"You doing okay?" My best friend, once Army brother, and current club brother, Deck asked me as we stood there waiting on my bride-to-be to actually show her ass up.

"What do you think?"

"Aw man, I know there's some bad blood because of how everything went down, but haven't you guys at least talked it out some?" Deck was the lying bitch's brother-in-law. That made him a little biased and hopeful that I would step up and be the better man. I was supposed to bury the hatchet on her lies and actually give this farce of a marriage a try.

I turned narrowed eyes on him instead. "I haven't spoken to her since she broke the news about the baby that day in the clubhouse," I admitted. Deck's eyes rounded out and he stepped back, almost as if I had physically assaulted him.

EIGHT WEEKS AGO

Deck had finally convinced me that I needed to quit slamming shit around, being angry, and get over his little sister-in-law and the trap she had made me fall for. It had been a little over a month since I found out that she was really a club princess, that everyone called her Anna instead of Lise. Granted, her full name was Annalise, but that didn't help ease her deception at all. I also, God help me, found out she was under age by the club standards and my own personal standards too, the law be damned.

I ended up on this double date with Ever and Deck as a result. The woman wasn't too hard to deal with, but that spark I had felt with Anna all those times we had been together just wasn't there. Hell, I didn't know if I'd ever feel anything like it again. Anna had been a magic balm to my soul, and one I hadn't known I needed until she was ripped away from me and her lies exposed.

Mindy had been Deck's pick. Apparently, he knew her from high school so she was far more age appropriate than the girl who had my mind swirling from want to need to anger and back again. I couldn't fault his choice, physically speaking. He had obviously tried to go in a different direction with looks. The bitch was blond with blue eyes and tits for days. She also had a bit more weight on her everywhere else than Anna did, but I supposed that was the difference in Anna still very much being a teenager and Mindy being a full-fledged woman.

Mindy didn't seem to have a shy bone in her body and took to me like a fly to shit. It was exactly the thing that turned me off in women when it came to dating. I didn't like the over eager aggressive types. I preferred… Well, my preference hadn't seemed to do me a whole lot of good. Anna had been the epitome of my preference. Mild-mannered, shy, reserved, and willing to let me take the lead was my type. I didn't want to lord over my woman. I just didn't want one who thought she could pull all of my strings, and manipulate me on purpose like I was nothing more than a puppet on a string.

Mindy was not shy. By the time dinner was over, she had touched my dick at least four times, and then pouted when she realized I wasn't an uncontrolled boy popping a boner at every look or touch from a woman. She played it off each time as if it were an accident, but we both knew better. That was my other distinct turn off with women. The ones who played games were not meant for me. This one was a game player from the word go.

"I need to grab my cell," Deck mentioned as we left the restaurant. I left it at the clubhouse earlier when we were there. You mind swinging in there?"

"I don't mind," I told him as we all moved to my truck.

"Oh goodie!" Mindy chirped as she hopped in the passenger side, leaving Ever and Deck to climb in the back. "That means we can ditch this old truck and pick up your bikes. I want to go for a ride!"

I didn't know how to break it to her, but the bitch wasn't getting on the back of my bike. I'd only had one woman on it, and I didn't plan on putting another there. I was about to tell her just that when Ever perked up in the back.

"That sounds like a plan. I love a night ride, but the sun will be setting soon. If we get to the clubhouse quick enough, it will be perfect. We can head towards the beach and then the moon should be up by the time we cruise on down…" the rest of what she was saying was lost to me. I couldn't believe she was sitting here planning out a romantic sunset/moonlit ride for her sister's ex-boyfriend and another woman. What the fuck was wrong with Ever? I glared at her through my rearview mirror and I watched as the bitch smirked at me. She fucking smirked. She knew exactly what she was doing.

It was then I resigned myself to having Mindy on the back of my bike just so Ever could see how far her plan was about to blow up in her face. Deck may have had friendly intentions trying to get me to go out with someone else and take my mind off of things, but his meddling woman was attempting to be pull some shit.

We pulled up and went around to the back of the clubhouse instead of heading in the front because Deck thought he left his cell in the kitchen and we didn't want anyone holding us up from this ride we were about to take.

"You know, all those vibrations from your bike are bound to get me super horny, right?" Mindy asked. I watched as Ever rolled her eyes and Deck tried not to laugh.

"Have you ever ridden on a bike before?" I asked the woman.

"Well, no, but I've heard…" she started to say.

"Oh, my bike will get your motor revving for sure, just be sure that's what you really want before you hop on the back of my bike." I turned so that my eyes met Ever's then. Two could play her fucking game. "I'm in the market for a new old lady, so play your cards right, it might not be the only ride you get."

Deck cut his eyes to me then before glancing over at his wife. Understanding dawned and he shook his head. "Not in front of my virginal ears, kids!" He joked while covering his ears like a child would when they don't want to hear something. We all laughed as Ever opened the back door and walked inside. She halted in her tracks giving us just enough space to all pile in tightly behind her. I was about to ask what was up when she entertained a question of her own that pulled my focus forward.

"Momma-Luce? Anna?" My attention shifted to the two women that were standing in the back hall along with Double-D. I had thought that he and Lucy hadn't made up yet, but then again I didn't know shit about that family that I thought I did. "What's going on?" Ever's question mirrored my own thoughts.

The hallways was quiet as the grave for a moment before Anna bit into her bottom lip, worrying it with her teeth before just blurting out two words that sunk me. "I'm pregnant." I felt the blood drain from my face as they penetrated my suddenly fogged brain. She was what now? Pregnant? By who?

"Shit!" Deck called out.

"Isn't that your little sis, Ev?" Mindy asked as she moved closer, thrusting her tits into my arm as she grabbed onto my bicep in a tight hold. I didn't know if she realized Anna's pregnancy announcement might have something to do with me or not, but it sure as fuck felt like this bitch I had just met was trying to mark territory. Unfortunately, I was still trying to wrap my stupefied brain around those two life altering words. "We better leave them to the family stuff. Looks like it's gonna get brutal." I didn't miss the hopeful edge to her tone. This bitch was hungry for the family's drama for some reason.

"You will go nowhere!" Double-D shouted and the bitch stopped tugging on my arm trying to get me back out of the door behind us. Double-D looked Mindy over, finding her lacking by the disgust that was clear to read, and then he shifted his focus to me. "I see it didn't take you long to move on from my daughter after knocking her up," he roared, sounding like a feral damn bear.

"The fuck!" I yelled back, finally amassing a little clarity that allowed me to think past the too-fast beat of my heart. "I didn't even know she was pregnant. You told me to stay away from her! She lied about who the fuck she was and how old she was, and who knows what else she lied about too. Probably everything. Probably lying about being pregnant too, for all I know. What did you expect me to do? Sit around, pining for a liar who never told me she was pregnant to begin with?"

"Ever," Double-D called out, ignoring my tirade. "Get her out of here, please." He tipped his chin toward the woman still clinging to my arm as if someone was about to take away her favorite toy. As if she was used to having me as her toy. The image she portrayed was more than of the two of us being out on our first date. I was still unable to even so much as glance over at Anna. If I looked at her now, it would be real. Her words would be real and I would have to deal with them. Just a little longer, and…

"No!" Mindy had the audacity to yell at Double-D. "I came

with Joker, and I'm going to leave with him."

"You sure as fuck aren't talking to my family like that!" Ever yelled at her as she yanked on my other arm pulling me free from Mindy's unexpecting clutches. "I don't give a fuck if Joker wants that pussy, we'll chalk this one up to him losing out." I don't know if it was the shock of Ever saying something like that in front of her family, or what, but the entire room grew still as the tomb. Then I watched Ever's horrified face as she turned to her sister. "Shit!" She proclaimed, and then mumbled out a quick apology to Anna who I couldn't avoid looking at any longer. Her beautiful face was contorted in a mask of pain as a tear slipped free from her long lashes and fell freely down her cheek. My heart clenched at the sight.

"What in the fuck is happening to my family?" Double-D asked while losing some of his bluster. Ever turned venomous eyes on Mindy, but Deck stepped in the way pointing his finger to someone beyond my view. "Prospect there is gonna show you the way out and see that you get home," he told Mindy.

"Yeah, whatever," she responded snidely. "Joker, I like you, but I'm not trying to raise anyone else's babies for them just because their baby mamma is too young to do it."

"Fuck you!" Anna shouted as I watched Double-D reach for and take hold of his daughter before she could launch herself at Mindy's smug face. "You're not coming anywhere near my baby, Bitch!"

"Holy fuck!" I'd been shocked as shit to hear those words come from Anna's mouth, especially the way they were laced with so much venom. Come to think of it, that was both the first and the last time I ever heard Anna cuss.

"Come on," Double-D called out to everyone, and then seemed to think better of the order. "Actually, just you," he said to me. Something was communicated silently between Ever and her father in the next minute before Anna stopped it.

"It's okay. I'd rather you be there, Ever."

"If that's what you want," she agreed.

Surprisingly enough, Double-D ended up leading all of us to the room that the club used for Church. This was a place women weren't supposed to be allowed to enter at all and now it was filled with Double-D's family, which included his wife and two daughters.

"You want me to wait out here?" Deck asked.

"Why? You're family too," Anna informed Deck, as if he didn't already know he'd married into this craziness.

When we were seated, it didn't escape my attention that I had been basically surrounded by Anna's family with Double-D sitting on one side of me while Deck was to my other. Anna and Lucy were seated across from us. It was as if they all thought they had to trap me in the room in order for me to do the right thing by her, or whatever their end goal was here.

"I'm assuming since you're here with her, the pregnancy was

21

confirmed?" Double-D asked as he glanced down at Anna's hands that were hiding under the table. "I saw what you were holding," he informed her.

She glanced up at her dad with unshed tears glimmering in her eyes still. Then her face broke out in the most beautiful smile I'd ever seen on her. There had to be a hidden path from heaven to the girl's soul, because there was no way a person could light up like that without some sort of divine intervention. I froze, unable to move as I just took the sight of her in and contemplated how someone so perfect could have been so devious in her pursuit of me, so selfish as to nearly cost me everything I'd worked for since I left the Army, and callous enough to rip my heart out with the truth of her betrayal.

"Before you found out who she was, how did you feel about my daughter?" The question from Double-D took me aback and jolted me out of my reverie, but he was already moving on to the next question before I could even register what he was saying. "How long were you seeing one another? Were you seeing one another or did you just think she was nothing more than club pussy since she was hanging around?" What the fuck kind of shit was this asshole spouting off about his own daughter? I got to my feet, and then I put the mother fucker on his back with a punch to his jaw. Fuck that guy. How dare he speak about his own kid that way?

"CJ!" Lucy's shrill cry of her husband's name didn't faze me one bit.

"You talk like that about your own daughter?" I screamed at him as Deck moved around me to help him up. The bastard started laughing at me as he moved to pick himself up from the floor.

"Now you're laughing?" I asked. He glanced around at everyone and smiled at Ever who was also smirking, a knowing look passed between the two of them, and all the while the fucker didn't stop laughing. My fingers twitched with the itch to throttle the bastard. "You're seriously sitting there laughing after insinuating your daughter is a whore? What the fuck, man? No wonder your family's falling apart and your kid's acting out. Jesus. She told me her family was fucked since her brother died." I turned to see Anna's face scrunch in sadness as I spilled one of her secrets to her family. "I see that now." I couldn't keep looking at her though, so I shifted my focus back to her father. "She told the truth about something, at least."

Double-D took his time getting to his feet. He then massaged his jaw with his hand before turning a dopey grin on me. I took an inadvertent step backwards, because that grin was so fucking off-putting I didn't know what might come out of the man next. I could see a plan forming in his eyes and I had a good feeling about where this shit was going.

"Looks like we need to set up a good ol' southern shotgun wedding, son!" It wasn't long after his declaration, and the gasps of surprise had died down from two of the three women present, that Lucy scooped Anna up into arms and took them out of the room, leaving me with her father, Deck, and Ever to go over the details of my impending nuptials.

WEDDING DAY

"Are you fuckin' serious?"

"As a heart attack, brother," I answered him and turned back around to stare at the cracked gray wall once more. Deck moved away from me and off to the side where his wife, the very sweet and beautiful Ever, stood waiting for things to get a move on too. She seemed almost disinterested in the events playing out now until Deck said something to her. The shock on her face was easy to read. I guess her little sis had been spitting more lies about her impending nuptials and the part I was playing in them. I really couldn't expect any less, I guess. She lied about everything. Hell, if her mother hadn't been there to confirm the sonogram pictures, I would have thought she was lying about the baby too.

I know what you're probably thinking. Why the hell am I going through with this if I hate her so much? In this day and age, you don't have to be married to co-parent. I know this. The thing is, I was medically discharged from the military. I get medical coverage for life now. That means my future wife and kids will also be covered. A DNA test was done when Anna got an amnio done. The kid was mine, though I wasn't allowed to know if it was a boy or a girl even though I knew the test would show the sex. Anna didn't want to know, so I didn't get to know.

Getting the DNA test had been one of my stipulations before agreeing to marry her. I would stay married to Anna to make sure she remained covered by my insurance through the pregnancy and post-partum crap. Most likely, we'd finalize our divorce after that, but the baby would still be covered by me even if it's mom wasn't any longer. Hopefully, by then I'd have a plan about what to do concerning the baby, and the fact that this bitch's lies had ruined how I had pictured my future life. I was supposed to get married once – maybe, but it was supposed to be with the person who birthed my kid, and it was supposed to be for life. I didn't want a bunch of different bitches out there giving birth to a hoard of my children like some men did. I wanted shit to be normal – something I didn't have growing up.

Fucking hell. Too bad I didn't think to tell her that I didn't want her lies ruining my life when we met. Hindsight – she is a bitch. I glanced down at the watch I wore. I'd been standing here wasting this man's time for 45 minutes now. I glanced around to see that Ever had left the room and Deck was standing in back looking worried. I was fuckin' done.

I started walking back down the little aisle that had been created by the few fold out chairs that had been brought in so the witnesses had a place to sit. "What's up?" Deck asked as I drew closer to him.

I glanced at my watch once more. "What's up? Really? I've been waiting 45 fuckin' minutes for this shit-show to get started. I'm done. They can come find me another day, when I'm not busy, and not being held up by their lying daughter doing God knows what in order to make her grand entrance."

I heard the gasp and we both looked to the doorway where Double-D was standing with his daughter's hand in the crook of his arm. She was wearing a pretty little ivory dress with peach flowers all over it. It fit tight to her much larger than they used to be tits and the baby bump she now had while swishing around her legs down just above her knees. Her long, dark brown hair was pulled back on the sides and the curled length draped down behind her shoulders to disappear behind her back. Tears wrecked what I was guessing had been the perfect make-up job. Then there was her dad, spitting hellfire and brimstone at me. Well shit.

I watched as Anna tried to remove her hand from her father's arm to no avail. He held her captive there in the doorway. He pointed a single finger toward the man waiting to marry us and I complied with a shrug of my shoulders. What did it actually matter to me anyway? I was marrying her for one reason only beyond the insurance shit. It would mean easier access to my kid, and the ability to get all the dirt I needed on her when it came time to go to court over custody because there would definitely be a time for that.

"Daddy, no, please. This is humiliating enough." I don't know what she thought she had to be humiliated about. I was the one who had been deceived, not her.

"Anna, you made your bed," I heard him say to her. Here I was thinking he was trying to punish me with this marriage bullshit, but honestly I was beginning to think this was just his way of pushing another kid out the door. I felt a twinge of guilt for thinking that considering they'd all lost Toby not too long ago. Double-D's son had been a club brother, or he would have been if he'd lived long enough to see me patched in officially. He was a decent guy, and I hated like hell that I knew at least part of what Anna had told me about losing her brother had been true. The emotion she had shown when she spoke of him is what had clawed at my heart and made me give her a chance. She was a horrible fuckin' human if that had all been a part of her game too.

"Short version is just fine," Double-D told the judge as he stood his daughter up beside me. The both of us refused to look at each other and instead chose to focus on the man marrying us.

The judge glanced back and forth a couple times between me and my sobbing bride-to-be. Then his eyes moved to Double-D. "You know we don't really have to do this anymore for those in her condition."

"It's getting done," Double-D returned and then stood quietly behind us. I guess he was there just in case one of us tried to pull a runner. I was fuckin' tempted. I didn't really need the club, did I? Fuck. Despite how badly I didn't want to marry this girl now that she had shown me her true self, nothing could stop me from wanting to be there for my own kid. I knew what it was like to live without the love of one of your parents. Instead of running, I stood there and swore vows to the woman who had put us both in this position by lying her ass off to me. I didn't expect her to hold steady to her vows, considering she was untrustworthy already at best. I certainly hoped she didn't plan on me doing any better. I was there for my kid, she was just incidental shit to deal with. This was a contract we were signing so that health insurance would cover her, and nothing more. I continued to tell myself that as I tried too damn hard not to see the way her shoulders shook as she cried beside me.

Chapter 2

I was married. There had always been this illusion in the back

of my mind that when I finally got married one day, I would feel

different somehow. Complete. Having met the other half of my

soul and tied myself to him for the rest of our lives was supposed

to mean something. It was supposed to make me feel different.

All I felt sitting in the passenger side of Joker's truck as he drove

us away from the courthouse was infinite sadness. He hated me

and, what was worse, I couldn't blame him for it one bit. I had

lied to him about who I was and how old I was. It was something that could have ruined his life, and I'd done it out of selfishness. It hurt my heart to think of what kind of person that made me. I rubbed the little baby belly I was starting to get and knew it didn't matter anymore because I could never regret anything that made my child.

Still, it was hard for me to even look over at my husband. That word didn't bring elation like I once dreamed it would. Instead, it felt false rolling around my head. I'd probably never say it out loud, because we weren't really married. He'd made that clear when he refused to supply wedding rings, or even kiss me when the Justice of the Peace told him he could. No, what we were was a business transaction on paper only. The tears burning my eyes threatened to spill over again. I refused to let him see any more of them though. When the clubhouse came into view, I finally glanced his way. I thought we'd been headed to his house so he could show me around and I could get settled in.

Of course, there had been no plans for a honeymoon. I didn't think there would be, but I hadn't been prepared for being dragged to the clubhouse where I would undoubtedly be humiliated by being the 'blushing bride' paraded around even though he'd been reluctant to marry me. Reluctant probably wasn't a strong enough word, actually. I knew the way the guys at the club gossiped about one another's lives. They already knew this was a sham of a wedding and only being done because

THE PRINCESS *and the* PROSPECT

I was pregnant and... Yeah, so it was going to be humiliating.

When we parked, Joker didn't bother to say a word to me. Instead, he got out of his truck and took off toward the clubhouse, leaving me there to sit in the truck. He didn't even offer the courtesy of helping me down out of the truck that was way too high for me. I sighed and opened the door, but before I could contemplate jumping down my father's friend, Crow, was there. "Come on little lady, let me help you out. You shouldn't be hopping around when you're in your condition." He helped me down and then glanced around the parking lot finding it empty of any other people. "Were you supposed to wait here for Joker?"

I shrugged my shoulders. "He didn't say what we were doing here. He just went inside." I told him as my face heated with embarrassment at having to admit that my now husband couldn't even offer me that courtesy, never mind the help getting out of his monster of a truck.

Crow gave me an odd look before he pulled me into his arms and hugged me tightly. "Everything will be okay, Princess. It'll get better. You guys just need some time to adjust."

A bitter laugh erupted from my dry throat, nearly making me choke on the coughing fit it produced. Crow squeezed me tighter. "It's kind of you to say anyway," I told him before peeling myself out of his arms and moving towards the clubhouse door.

"You have my number, if you need anything, you just call. You hear me?"

"You're not coming in?" I asked Crow, worried that none of the older crowd would be there to take my back in case things got dramatic or out of hand.

"No, honey. I was on my way out just now."

"Okay, well see you around," I told him and turned my back as quickly as possible because once again those tears were starting to burn my eyes. I knew what my dad said to me earlier today was true enough. I'd done this to myself and there was no use crying about it. More to the point – if I needed to cry, I would have to do it where no one could see.

Once I pushed the door open, the only way to describe the scene was loud. The music – it sounded like something from Disturbed – was cranked up so loud I couldn't even hear my own thoughts. I could make out some laughter and yelling from across the room though. I glanced around and noticed that Joker was standing by the pool table talking to another newer member that I hadn't gotten to know yet. There were a few women standing around with them too, which I found strange, because I thought – after what happened with Toby – that they weren't allowed to be here anymore. I shook off the thought and moved over to the bar to park my ass on a stool until Joker was ready to take me to his house. The prospect behind the bar gave me a pitying look before leaning in to ask what he could get for me.

"Can you just get me a ginger ale?"

"Sweetheart, we don't have that back here. You want a Sprite or something?"

"Sure," I mumbled, my stomach feeling even queasier then.

He slid a glass my way and plopped a straw down in it as he did so. "I'm not sure it's my business to say anything, but this doesn't look like the kind of place where a pregnant lady should be hanging out," he offered up as he glanced down at my slightly rounded belly. I just shrugged my shoulders.

"Looks like I'm stuck here for a while."

I watched as Joker finished off a bottle of beer and tossed the empty into the trashcan near the pool table. Then he swatted one of the girl's asses and she turned to head to the bar. She stood right beside me as she ordered two beers. One was for her and the other was for Joker. I knew the second was for him because as soon as she had them in hand, she gave me a quick smile and took off for the other side of the room and handed it to him while leaning her body into his. She was a pretty redhead with long legs and curves in all the right places. She wasn't overly done like some of the fake women that used to creep around this place, but still. It was obvious she was flirting with him and getting cozy. She probably didn't know he'd come straight here from getting married to me. I wondered if he would even tell her that he had. He didn't seem to care that her boobs were pressed into his side, and the amount he cared about the display was proven when he threw his arm around her and pulled her closer. She leaned in, giggling, and I turned around, unable to see anything else without bawling my eyes out.

Seeing my empty drink the prospect smiled at me. "Can I get you another?"

I shook my head knowing that if I overdid it with the soda, I would have to pee – a lot – and I didn't want to have to walk past the man I'd only just married as he carried on with another woman hanging all over him.

"Is there anything else I can get for you? Are you waiting for anyone in particular? Need me to call someone for you?" The prospect rambled off the list of questions, obviously uncomfortable with having to deal with me sitting at the bar.

"Nope," I told him. Then I gave him my full attention. "I'm waiting on Joker. He's supposed to take me to his house at some point."

The prospect gave me a doubtful look. "He's working on his fourth beer at this point." He pointed over to the small crowd that had gathered around the man in question. "Looks like they're starting in on the shots too. Are you sure he knows you're supposed to be going to his house later?" I could see why he was doubting me since Joker had traded out the redhead from earlier and now had a brunette wrapped around him, dancing on him like he was her own personal stripper pole.

"I'm pretty sure that's where he was supposed to take me."

"Do you need me to take you there instead? I'm sure I could get someone to cover for me for a little bit."

I shook my head, blushing with embarrassment once again. What did that make? At least five times today so far? I made a noise in the back of my throat that signified how fed up I was with the fact that I kept having to play off my own embarrassment. "I don't have a key yet. He was supposed to have all that taken care of for me today."

The prospect gave me a dubious look then. "Are you sure?"

I sighed. "Well, I was when he brought me here. Now, I don't know, but either way I have nowhere else to go for now."

"There isn't anyone else you can call?"

"No one else cares," I informed him. That probably wasn't exactly true. I could call my mom or Ever and they would be here to get me in a heartbeat. I just didn't want to see their faces when, less than a few hours into my marriage, I admitted defeat and asked to be bailed out. My father's words echoed through my head once more. "You made your bed…" he kept saying every time he even caught wind of me complaining about the morning sickness I'd endured, or the tears I'd cried because pregnancy hormones were kicking my ass.

He wasn't saying it to be cruel, just to make me face the reality of my situation, and he was right. I had made this bed, and now I was watching as other women were about to lie in it while I was forgotten on the sidelines on my wedding day. Two hours went by at a sluggish pace considering I wasn't one of the party revelers who was having fun. Time was probably speeding by like a bullet train for them. It was weird how all that worked. I had finally relented and had another soda and then some water. I needn't have worried about drawing Joker's attention as I made my way to the bathroom though because he didn't notice any of the three times I made the trip down the back hallway that was situated just past the pool tables. Instead, I'd managed to get all the way back to the bar to be offered yet another pitying look from the prospect who was fetching more drinks as the number of people attending this particular party picked up.

"Are you sure I can't take you home, or to someone who you can stay with until Joker…" The prospect, who appeared to be leaving now, asked as he glanced over his shoulder. I wasn't sure what he'd been about to say though. Until Joker remembers you're alive? Until he sobers up? Who knows. It was all the same thing anyway. Obviously, I wouldn't be getting back in that truck with him tonight. Not that I'd risk myself to riding with someone who was drinking and driving, but I definitely wasn't about to risk my baby. I shook my head at the man.

"No. If it goes too much later, I'll see if I can borrow a room for the night."

"No offense lady, but the rooms are for the brothers and visiting guest, not chicks that were brought here and forgotten," he countered. I knew he didn't intentionally mean to be cruel because I watched as his face flushed. "I didn't…"

I held my hand up. "It's okay. I get why you'd think the worst," I told him as I glanced back at Joker, who now had two women hanging on him. I pointed in their direction. "It certainly doesn't seem like I am someone who would need a room here tonight, unlike Joker there. I'm Anna, Double-D's daughter," I finally divulged. The prospect's eyes went wide.

"Shit, I'm sorry. I didn't realize. Does he know you're here? Do you need me to call him?" He cautiously glanced back at Joker then. "Does he know Joker's supposed to be your ride?"

"He knows, and I don't need you to call him. Thank you though, for checking on me. I'll be sure to tell daddy how nice you were to me."

I could see the relief in the man as his shoulders slid back down from where they were darn near plastered to his ears with tension. I smiled brightly at him and wished him a good night. I noticed him texting someone on his phone before he walked out, but other than a brief glance back at me and a quick wave of his hand, he was gone and I was left there at the bar utterly alone for the first time all night. Sure, there were people hanging around, but none of them even bothered giving me a second glance, let alone caring about what might happen to me tonight.

When I turned my attention back to the pool tables, my stomach rolled and tumbled with the sight that greeted me. Joker had his hand wrapped in a blond woman's hair and the other

37

firmly holding her waist close to his own. Their lips were locked in a steamy kiss that seemed to go on forever. Her hands were each buried in a back pocket of his jeans and his hair. The clinch they were in was more along the lines of what I'd expected at my own wedding when the Justice of the Peace informed Joker he could now kiss his bride. Instead, I was given the cold shoulder, and now I was forced to watch as he gave that kiss to another woman, and did it right in plain sight of me. If I thought anything else in this messed up day had hurt me, I'd been wrong, because nothing could top what I was feeling in that moment.

Glancing down at the glass of water in my hand I suddenly wished, for a moment, that I wasn't pregnant because then I could drink this day away too. Then again, if I wasn't pregnant, this day wouldn't exist. I could have mourned the loss of Joker early on and then moved on with my life. Eventually. Instead, I had that image emblazoned on my mind as the only kiss that happened on my wedding night. My lips were doomed to be lonely for a long time, it seemed.

"Anna?" I glanced up to see my father's best friend – Merc – standing there watching me cautiously. "What are you doing here so late, honey? Aren't you supposed to be staying at Joker's house?" He glanced around then and stiffened as he took in the site I was about to be sick from watching. Joker was still going at it hot and heavy with the blond. "Fucking hell, I'll kill the bastard." He moved, as if to go after Joker then, but I placed my hand on his arm to still him.

"Please, don't do that. He didn't marry me because he loved me. I already know that," I reasoned.

"Honey, even if I thought for a minute you were okay with sharing your new husband with other women – and for the record I do not believe that – he has no business leaving you here this late at night like this. Especially not when he's allowing you to witness this bullshit on top of knowing you're pregnant with his child." Merc shook his head, as if he could just make the anger disperse that way. "Told Double-D this was a bad fucking idea," he mumbled under his breath. "Come on, I'm going to take you home with me. Tiger Lily will be there if you need someone to talk to about all this. Honestly though, I'm guessing you could use the rest. You look dead on your feet."

"I am sleepy," I told him needlessly when I was overcome by a yawn that wouldn't be contained. I hopped up off of the bar stool and moved to head in Joker's direction.

"Where are you going?"

"I just want to let him know where I'll be so he won't worry."

"No!" Merc was adamant in his response as he grabbed hold of my upper arm and started moving me toward the door of the clubhouse. "Let's allow him to stew in that worry. Honestly, I don't expect him to remember you were even here until sometime tomorrow anyway."

My lower lip trembled and, for the first time in hours, I found myself trying really hard not to cry again. "He forgot me before I ever even made it in the building after him," I admitted. I glanced back once to see he was still wrapped up in the blond woman's presence and her arms. My heart plummeted into my stomach all over again at the sight. This was not the marriage I had always dreamed of having as a girl. I could have dealt with the shitty wedding, but I never thought for a minute that my own husband would cheat on me on our wedding night, and do it so blatantly in front of me.

Then again, it was made painfully obvious that he had been oblivious to my presence. So, maybe he hadn't put on the blatant display for me, but it was just as bad that he'd forgotten about his pregnant wife being there, let alone being alive somewhere. He wasn't concerned about hurting me or making a fool of me either. I guess I deserved the latter since he felt I'd made a fool of him not long ago when I didn't tell him my full name or correct his assumptions about my age. I didn't do it to be hurtful to him or play games though – as he'd accused me of doing. I did it because for once, I wanted something for myself without who my family was taking it away from me. I sighed as I tucked myself in on the back of Merc's motorcycle and hung on to him as he sped us away to his house. My bag was forgotten in Joker's truck. The only thing I had in my possession now was the cell phone in my back pocket. I hoped like heck it didn't fall out onto the ground as we rode, but honestly who would be calling me anyway? Not my husband, that was for sure.

Chapter 3

"What the fuck?" I heard Deck yell as someone shook me awake. My whole body throbbed and felt off kilter with all the alcohol I had consumed. There was also a heavy weight bearing down on my chest that was pushing what remained of the alcohol in my stomach right up into my esophagus with an acidic burn from hell that was going to lead to me puking sooner rather than later.

"I should kick your ass right now," Deck was screaming at

me. "But I want you to feel it and remember every single punch, mother fucker."

"What are you on about?" I grumbled just as the weight on my chest shifted and my hand landed on a juicy, naked ass that I just couldn't keep my hand from squeezing. Maybe being married wouldn't be so bad if Anna was gonna wake me up like this every morning. My dick sprung wood at the thought.

"You can't be serious right now. You're really doing this? In front of me? In front of Ever?"

Well, he had a point there. "Anna babe, get up," I called out to my new wife, who I realized had to be the one draped over me and causing me to want to vomit. Not because I didn't like having her weight on me, but after the drinking I'd done, it wasn't going to end pretty. Besides, there was the audience we had obviously collected standing by to see her body which I didn't like to think about one bit. "Come on, Anna. Your bro shouldn't be seeing your ass."

I heard Ever scoff. "That's rich!" She huffed those words out, though I still hadn't opened my eyes to see why because my eyelids felt like sandpaper already in their closed position. I knew it would hurt when I finally managed to open them. "You deal with this shit, Deck. I've got to find my sister. She's probably devastated right now. Jesus, I can't even imagine."

"Anna," I fussed again, smacking the ass under my hand.

"That's not Anna, you stupid fucking prick!" Deck screamed

at me causing my head to pound dramatically.

"Baby, it's Stacey, remember?" A strange feminine voice cooed near my ear. I jerked away from the sound and finally managed to prise my eyes open enough to see the blond hair that was in my face.

"What the fuck?" I pushed the bitch off of me.

"You told me to cuddle up with you after I sucked you off last night," she said as her bottom lip poked out in a pout. She had remnants of red lipstick smeared on her face and I glanced down to see that my dick was still hanging out of my pants and, sure as fuck, there was a red ring around it that matched this bitch's lipstick. No. "Oh, fuck no!" I moaned out loud.

"Yeah, asshole." Deck confirmed what I was seeing. I had forgotten for a moment that he was there until he spoke up again. "Got your dick wet with some strange bitch on your wedding night while your pregnant, 17-year-old wife probably had a front row seat to you doing it. Once you wrap your head around that, maybe you can pull the stick out of your ass and realize people fuck up, and what you just did – it makes her mistake pale in comparison.

"Fucking hell," I grumbled as I tucked my dick away inside my pants.

"Now, where the fuck is my little sister-in-law? You were supposed to get her settled in at your place last night, asshole."

I tried to remember, but couldn't place the last time I'd been aware of Anna. Maybe on the ride from the courthouse to the club? "Maybe she went back to her parent's house?"

"Are you shittin' me right now?"

"I don't fuckin' know. We got in the truck after that bullshit fucking wedding and I was so fucking lost…" I glanced around, and when everything seemed too fuzzy and started to spin I just glanced back down at my own lap. "I don't even remember getting here. I don't know where Anna is. Did you check my truck?"

"Who the hell are you, man? There's a pregnant, scared, heartbroken girl out there somewhere and you can't remember anything? I don't know what you did with my buddy, but it'd be great to have him back instead of this asshole before me." He turned to walk away.

"Where are you going?" I asked, even knowing my voice was filled with panic.

"Someone has to find Anna and make sure she and your baby are okay, fucker."

"Check with Lucy," I managed to get out.

"She ain't there!" He yelled the words back at me. "She wasn't with me and Ever. She's gone, and since you never took her to your place, I'm guessing she ain't there either. That means she had no-fucking-where to go. Did you ever give her a key to your house? The address even?" At the near blank look on my face, save for the guilt I knew he could see, I had no answers.

"Did you even give her your new phone number?"

He could see by my reaction that I hadn't. Truth be told, I hadn't even thought about the fact that I'd changed the number when I was angry with her. She had texted me several times, apologizing profusely in each one and I couldn't stand to look at them any longer. So, I had changed the number. Deck shook his head at my obvious non-response. He was completely disgusted with me and not hiding it one bit. I felt the same about myself in that moment.

"She's 17 and she made a mistake while trying to live her life outside the shadow of the club. She just wanted to be a normal girl who had a regular boy she liked. I get why she did it. It makes sense, even if it hurt you, because you only saw your side of things. Your wounded pride is keeping you from seeing hers though. You are a grown man. This shit you pulled on that girl's wedding night? She will never be able to forget this. So help me, if she's hurt or that baby is, I will never forgive this."

What could I say to that? He wasn't wrong. I was starting to see just how wrong I might have been about everything that went down with Anna. I'd never bothered to think about why she had done it. I just assumed she thought it was cute to play games with the prospect even though it never felt quite right to think that.

"What do I do? I have no clue where she is." He could see the misery written on my face, self-inflicted though it was.

"I don't know there's anything you can do at this point. The whole scene Ever and I walked in on this morning was a situation there isn't a whole lot of coming back from. I know you lost my respect and I'm not so certain Ever will speak to you again considering she just watched you disrespect her sister at your wedding yesterday and walked in to see you with some blond bitch draped on top of you and your dick still out?" He once again shook his head and then turned his back on me to walk away. "Find her sister. That might help. Considering Anna probably saw the shit you were up to last night, I'm guessing you have a lot more to atone for, and probably won't be able to do it. Hope you don't mind never seeing your kid, man. If I was her, I would make it impossible for you after that shit show."

I sighed, and knew there was one way to get answers. The club had video of the main room. I went in search of our security guy so I could find out what I'd been up to last night, and maybe get a lock on when Anna left and if she left with anyone. While it gave me some answers I might be able to work with to find Anna, I wished I hadn't forced myself to watch the tapes. Even fast-forwarding through most of the night I could see the devastation on Anna's face as she witnessed woman after woman pawing all over me as I did nothing to discourage it. Fuck.

Then I saw her turn to watch me making out with the blond I'd woken up with just a bit ago. I couldn't see her face to gage her reaction since she was at the corner of the camera's range and hidden partially by shadows, but one of the brother's came up to her at that point. He wasn't fully in view and I could only see the back of his kutte as he watched whatever she was looking at. The whatever being me with my tongue in another woman's mouth. The prospect behind the bar blocked my view when Anna left with a man's hand around her arm. My temper flared hot just thinking about another man dragging my woman out of the clubhouse last night, but then again, after what she witnessed, I guess I had that little sight coming to me.

Chapter 4

REPEATING
THE
PAST

efore I could move back into the shadows this time, he had

caught me watching him. My heartrate ticked up a few beats

per minute as the excitement kicked in. I wondered what he

would do. Would he come talk to me? Would he turn and give

all of his attention to the woman who had come in with another

brother? She seemed to be just as infatuated with him as I was.

They all laughed at something he said, though their voices didn't

carry to me where I sat on the sofa in the corner by myself. He

glanced back again and then snatched up the empty beer bottles that were scattered on the pool table.

He deposited the bottles into a large trash can on his way across the room. He was headed straight for me, but that couldn't be right. His light brown hair was still cropped close to his head on the sides and back, though he'd allowed the top to start growing out. It almost seemed like he needed baby steps to move on from the Army approved haircuts he had worn before. His face had likewise remained stubble free for the longest time. Though the past few times I'd seen him, there seemed to be a hint of a shadow across his well-defined jaw. His hazel eyes, that appeared mostly green up close and flecked with golden brown, were twinkling in amusement as he caught me staring once more. His movements hadn't been hindered at all by my watchfulness. If anything, he carried himself more securely the closer he came to where I sat.

I'd been watching him for months now, waiting to make my move until after I turned 18 just like Toby had told me to do. The thought of my brother tore at my insides, and I nearly chickened out and ran from the room. Toby wasn't here anymore though. He didn't get to make his dreams come true. What if I listened to him and the beautiful man I was obsessed with decided to start dating someone else? What if one of us died tomorrow? Nothing was promised to anyone. I don't think Toby had been alive long enough to learn that lesson. His dying is the only reason I did.

THE PRINCESS *and the* PROSPECT

"I've seen you here before," the prospect said to me as he drew closer. "You belong to someone?"

"I belong to no one," I told him.

He glanced around, eyes sweeping the room, stopping on every single woman in the place. Each one had been escorted there by one of the men of the club. "Women aren't allowed in the building without an escort any longer. You have to at least belong to someone for the day," he insisted.

I smiled at him. "I'm related to one of the brothers, distantly," I tacked on at the end. I knew he'd walk away and not even think twice about it if he knew I was a club princess and the vice president's daughter at that.

He grinned at that, nodding his head as if in approval. "What's your name, beautiful?"

I felt the blush rise up my chest and into my cheeks as he uttered that nickname for me. "A-A, it's Lise." I had been about to tell him it was Anna, but I worried he would know exactly who I was. Not many of the newer people were aware that my full first name was actually Annalise.

"Lise, I'm Evan," he told me as he moved to sit down right next to me. Our thighs and knees touched and there was no hiding the fact that proximity sent tingles through my body. He watched with a smirk on his face as gooseflesh appeared up and down my arms. "What are you doing sitting over here all by your lonesome?" He tapped on the notebook in my hand, my *journal.*

"I was writing."

"What kind of things do you write?"

I blushed again. "I don't know all sorts of things. Sometimes poetry, short stories, or just thoughts about my day."

"Is it a hobby or something you want to do with your life?"

"Honestly?" I asked him. He nodded his head, watching me as if he really wanted to hear the answer. He was the first person in my life who had ever asked me that question. "I want to be a novelist one day. I want to write the most epic story of all time."

"That's a hefty goal, and a highly debatable one unless you narrow it down a little. The Bible is arguably the greatest story ever told to some people. Harry Potter is for others. Then there's Gone with the Wind, Tom Sawyer, The Lord of the Rings, and…"

My laughter could not be contained. "Okay, I get it! I need to pick a genre and shoot for the top of the little niche I find myself in first."

"Now, she's thinking. Take over the entire literary world after you get a taste for the fame, fortune, and best sellers lists."

I sat dreamily staring off into space. "Yeah," I whispered.

"I believe you can do it. You have that fire in your eyes," he told me before he stood up. "I better get back to work before they fire me."

I giggled. "They're not going to fire you," I insisted.

"No, they'll just make me wear the prospect patch longer."

"Do you like the club so far?"

"Yeah, I do." He stood and started to move away from me, but not before glancing back one more time. "I like it a lot more now."

The man from my memories kept moving back to the pool table where our remembered first conversation slipped into my newest nightmare. Evan turned and winked at me before grabbing the blond by the pool table and kissing her like I dreamed of being kissed.

I woke in a cold sweat, my heart beating rapid-fire shots against my chest. It was like experiencing the elation of our new relationship all over again, only to have last night's betrayal shoved at me to rip another piece of my heart from by chest.

By the time I got settled in last night at Merc's house in their guestroom, it was just after two in the morning and I was both exhausted and heartbroken all over again. I had just been shown my room when my cell phone beeped with an incoming text. I glanced long enough to see who it was from and shook my head in the negative when Merc silently asked the question. Was it Joker? No, he probably still didn't even realize he'd brought me there with him, let alone the fact that he'd left me in his truck and forgotten about me.

He left me alone after that, and I stupidly opened the text from a girl I used to attend school with, Melody. When I opened her text, I wasn't expecting to see a picture, let alone that it would have been taken at the clubhouse last night. I hadn't even noticed that she had been one of the women in attendance there. Then again, I was preoccupied most of the night, and at least I knew she wasn't one of the many women hanging all over my husband.

It was now just after breakfast time as I sat staring at the damn photo again, and what it meant for my future. Actually, the damn thing brought to mind that saying about not being able to look away from a train wreck. It's that moment when you see the damning evidence in full color that your dreams will never come true, yet you can't manage to look away even though it's making you physically sick. That was how I felt in the morning light as I stared at the photo. I wished I never saw it. I had seen enough the night before. Having to then see that it absolutely did go further than just kissing felt like a hot knife was trying to slice me open from the inside out.

The picture Melody sent was of the blond woman I'd seen making out with Joker last night right before I left with Merc. She was on her knees in front of him – my husband – on our wedding night. He had his fingers tangled in her hair and his head thrown back in ecstasy. The angle was just tilted to the side enough that I could see it hadn't been faked. The woman on her knees in front of him had his dick in her mouth as her eyes were rolled up toward his face, seeking his approval or something.

Another big, fat tear slid down my cheek. "Isn't this your new husband?" the text that had accompanied the picture had said. I was sure Melody and all her friends were having a big laugh at my expense. None of them knew I was pregnant yet. They didn't know why I was getting married, only that I was, and I had opted to finish school online as a result. For just a second, I felt a glimmer of what Ever must have gone through back in high school, and I was thankful I wouldn't have to stick it out as long as she had. I wasn't sure I could handle going back considering I was pregnant and I didn't need the worst moments of my life thrown in my face on a daily basis for everyone else's amusement. I imagined that wouldn't do my little one any good to have me so stressed out.

Two knocks sounded on my door before it promptly opened and Tiger Lily moved into the space I was occupying. My mom's best friend glanced at my phone, my tears, and then she walked over and took the darn thing from me. I didn't even bother to hide what I was looking at. What was the point? Most of the younger crowd from the club was there last night. Even though I never saw her son J-Bird, I was sure he would hear all about it. So would Deck, and in turn the rest of my family. As if I needed to be further humiliated.

I watched as Tiger Lily glanced down at the image displayed

there. Her lips thinned noticeably as she pulled them tight, causing the little lines around her mouth to deepen. Her eyes narrowed briefly, in what could only be anger. Then she released a harsh breath before taking a seat next to me on the edge of the guest bed.

She handed my phone back to me as her eyes met mine. Unlike the prospect who had been waiting on me last night, there wasn't a drop of pity in her gaze. Then she spoke softly, but with a purpose. "Can I tell you a story?" Since she hadn't reacted the way I expected, I simply tipped my head up and down acknowledging that she could, in fact, tell me a story.

"If it's happier than the one I'm currently living, sure."

She gave me a half-hearted smile before she continued on. "It didn't start out that way, but it changed, eventually." She stared off into the empty space across the room, clearly not seeing the chair that sat there or all the decorative pillows I'd removed from the bed during the night when I'd attempted to sleep and they bothered me. Truth be told, breathing bothered me considering how my night had gone, but I had to admit I took it all out on those poor, undeserving pillows.

"I was young when I got pregnant with Deck. I was 16 and he was 18. We weren't seriously dating or anything even though I wished we were. I'd had a crush on that boy since I was 12-years-old. He lived across the street and I planned our wedding while he did his own thing, oblivious to me." I knew they had been young parents, but I hadn't realized they'd been that young.

"I knew right away what I meant to him after our first time together. It had been at a party, and we hadn't gone there together. Just one of those things where we ended up there. Anyway, he all but forgot me and our night together afterward. When I'd see him in passing it was like he looked right through me."

"I bet that hurt," I told her as she paused and glanced back at me. She nodded her head and I could see the pain of those memories still haunted her. The sadness was so evident in her eyes. In that moment, I ached for Tiger Lily.

"It hurt like you wouldn't believe," she said as she glanced back down at my phone I'd tossed on the bed between us. Unfortunately, it had landed screen up and the image of Joker and the woman who had been with him last night were still there. Suddenly, I was hating the fact that the screen hadn't timed out yet. "Actually," she spoke again, pulling my eyes from the horrible image. "I guess you would know exactly what that's like."

I made a noise of agreement in the back of my throat as I marveled at the fact that bonding over our tainted loves had me feeling truly like an adult for the first time in my life. "What happened?" Obviously, I knew she ended up with Merc and that they were still together today so it couldn't be so bad. Could it? Tiger Lily was one of the strongest women I knew. I figured she was about to tell me how to fight for your true love and never take the kind of shit she'd just seen on my cell phone.

"The day I finally worked up the courage to tell him I had gotten pregnant, I interrupted a make out session with a girl from school who I hated. I didn't realize the two of them had been dating before. They'd been so quiet about it the first time around. Apparently, she was trying to make sure her parents didn't find out she was dating the bad boy from the wrong side of the tracks. That's why they had broken up just before he was with me at that party." Oh man, my heart hurt for the younger version of Tiger Lily. I couldn't imagine walking in on the boy I was in love with and an enemy of mine from school while I had news about being pregnant. No way could I have gone through with telling him. I stopped her story, because I laughed at that thought.

"Sorry, I was just thinking I couldn't have dealt with a situation like that and managed to tell him anyway, but I guess I had to go through something similar too."

Lily patted my leg in comradery before she carried on with her tale. "The girl who he was with had always been a bitch to me. It hurt double that he was with her, of all people. He knew, or at least I was pretty sure he did, how mean she was. I almost walked away without telling him, but that bitch opened her mouth and said the worst thing. 'Oh, look honey, virgin Lily was probably hoping you'd pop her cherry for her since she's so in love with you.' The cow actually laughed at her own joke after she said that to me. I lost my temper and my damn mind for the first time ever in that moment. I told her, 'He already did and now I'm pregnant with his baby, honey!' Then I walked out to find my dad and Merc's dad standing there in the hallway. They definitely heard what I said. I was mortified all over again."

"You and Merc ended up married because of your dads?" I guessed at her situation, seeming somewhat similar to my own.

"You betcha!"

"But it all worked out. You had Jason and you're still together after all these years." I smiled as I told her what she'd already lived through.

"Ah, sweet girl, it ain't all sunshine and roses. Merc and me went down some dark paths to get here. He cheated – a lot – at first. I told myself I didn't care because I had Declan to care for and we were taken care of financially, but I went through a world of hurt. When I found out I was pregnant with Jason, I made a plan to leave Merc. I had caught him cheating again and the stress… Well, I cramped bad and I thought I was going to lose the baby as a result."

"Why did you stay?"

She shrugged her shoulders. "That was around the time your dad lost your mom for a while. I don't know if seeing Double-D go through that was what did it, but Merc changed. He stayed home more. He didn't come home smelling like perfume or with lipstick on him. And he started spending time with me even when Deck wasn't around." Lily smiled at some long-lost memory before she was ready to continue.

"The day Jason was born was the first day I felt like I had a real husband."

"I'm not saying things will be the same for you, but considering that picture, I am telling you that you need to decide what you can live with. What you can forgive. Forgetting will never be an option, especially since that picture was taken on your wedding night. Moving forward is tough. If you want this, you work for it and lay down your own ground rules for what you will and will not tolerate. You may have messed up by lying in the beginning, but that doesn't give him the right to treat you like a punching bag for it. He agreed to marry you because you're having his baby. Not so that he can keep beating you down."

"He'd never hit me," I argued, misunderstanding her meaning of punching bag.

"Seeing what you saw last night, and the picture you got in that message, wasn't a giant punch to the gut for you?"

I glanced away, unable to look her in the eyes then. The misery swamped me at the glaring accuracy of what she'd just described. "Yes," I finally answered meekly. "It was exactly like that."

"Sweet girl, there are many forms of abuse in this world, and I'm not saying that's Joker's norm. I am saying, if you stay, you need to put your foot down about things like that. The stuff you can't or won't tolerate needs to be discussed so that he doesn't turn a mistake into a bad habit that will slowly eat away at your soul, and probably his own too, whether he realizes it or not."

Tiger Lily gave me a lot to think about, and a different perspective as she was doing it. For a brief instant, I wondered if my life could turn out like hers where I end up with the man I'd wanted after all. The problem was, every time I closed my eyes, all I could see was his fingers wrapped around a blond head of hair. I twirled a finger around the now limp, messy chocolate brown lock that managed to slip free of my unkempt ponytail. I knew then that I couldn't stomach going through years of knowing he was cheating on me the way Tiger Lily had with Merc. I wouldn't survive something like that. I also didn't think I could bring myself to ask her how she had managed to get through it all. Maybe another day.

Chapter 5

The video hadn't been much of a help thanks to the fact that

it angled to a point where Anna had been mostly in the shadows at the end of the bar, and whoever had come up to speak to her had been lost in them. I had attempted to track down some friends of Anna, but no one knew who she was hanging out with, or how to contact anyone who may have helped her. Not that it really mattered since it was obviously a club brother she had walked out of here with. Everyone I had spoken to today had denied it was them though. No matter how much of an asshole I'd made of myself the night before, I didn't think any of my brothers would openly lie to me, especially since my wife was missing now.

I was about ready to pull my own damn hair out, going crazy with worry, when I heard Merc call from down the hall where his office was. "Joker!"

"I can't find Anna," I told him as I continued walking away.

"Joker! Office, now!" He called out, halting me in my tracks.

"But I," I started and was abruptly cut off by him yelling, "Now!"

I entered the office, too keyed up to take a seat. Instead I stood there a moment as he clicked away on his computer. Then I started pacing and chewing on my thumb nail, nearly losing patience by the time he gave the machine before him one final clicked and then directed his attention to me.

"Look, I don't know what this is about, but I'm really worried. I need to find Anna."

"Are you?" He asked. I didn't answer, because what the fuck kind of question was that to ask? "Where are you going to look for her?"

I blew out a breath in frustration. "I don't fuckin' know," I finally admitted. "Nobody really knows her. It's crazy. Even her family is clueless about where she could be. I thought she left with another brother, but everyone I've asked has said it wasn't them."

Merc nodded knowingly. "That girl is something special. Her whole life she's been a dreamer, but she also lives to make people smile. I think the only selfish thing, or out of character thing, I've ever seen her do was to hide her true identity from you so she could have something that was just for her, for once."

I winced, feeling his censure for how I'd been treating her. Deck had already dislodged my head from my ass earlier by telling me something similar.

"Did you enjoy your time with her before you knew her real name and age?"

"Yes, of course," I answered.

"Would you have been serious about the woman you thought you were getting to know?" His question took me aback because my immediate internal response was to scream an emphatic yes to the heavens. I thought she had been the one that I could settle down and start a family of my own with.

Instead of tipping my hat, I just went with an easier response. "I had thought about it, yeah."

"Did she actually lie to you about anything other than which part of her name was the most commonly used nickname, or when she didn't correct your assumptions about her age?"

"She didn't bother telling me about her family's involvement with the club either."

"Did you tell her all about your family, friends, and coworkers? Did you tell her the little details about them, like their names, where they worked, what clubs they might belong to?"

"No," I answered, seeing where he was going with this.

"No, so maybe you were getting to know each other at the same pace then? Maybe she wanted you to be able to give her a chance to know and like her without her baggage sending you running?" His eyebrows arched upward to emphasize his question.

"I know. I overreacted a bit. I get it."

Merc grinned at me, but allowed the grin to drop and a grim countenance took its place. "I don't think you do," he managed to say before I started to disagree. He cut me off immediately though. "I took her to my home and Tiger Lily put her to bed last night because she'd had to stand witness to exactly how far out of the park you hit that overreaction." His words, once again, had me wincing.

"On her wedding night, she had to deal with a reluctant, pissed-off groom, a baby in her belly, and then I came out to find her watching you with your tongue down another woman's throat at damn near two in the morning. The girl was about to drop from exhaustion and then she got that jolt of adrenaline from seeing her new husband with another woman. You did that shit right the fuck in front of her eyes. I don't think you can fathom the work my wife had to put in to soothe that girl. Not that it mattered. I don't think she ever managed to fall asleep even though she pretended to for our sakes." His eyes roamed the room before settling on a picture that sat on his desk.

"Lily and I started with a shotgun wedding too. I knew she had a crush on me and in my stupid youth, I took advantage of that when the girl I'd been seeing regularly, but in secret, went out of town and broke up with me so that if she met someone while she was away it wouldn't be cheating. I figured if it was good enough for her, it was good enough for me too. I was at a party that night, and Lily was there watching me from the corner. She was shy back then, even though she was an MC princess.

"I took her innocence, and knocked her up while doing it. Then I walked away and didn't even give her a second glance until the day she told me she was pregnant. I had already been back together with my girl at that point. My girl dropped my ass then and there. My dad, and hers, had heard her confession and next thing I knew I was getting married. Hadn't even managed to finish high school yet. I was also suddenly prospecting for her dad's club. I already rode a bike, and had thought about putting my hat in the ring, but I still wasn't sure. Part of me had been thinking about trying to make a go of it in the town where my girl had wanted to go to college instead.

"I didn't take the marriage seriously. Hell, I left her alone for the most part. We didn't even sleep together again until damn near almost a year after we were married. Deck had already been born by then. She knew I was cheating on her. She wouldn't touch me because of it. One night, my parents had Deck, and told me I needed to take her out because she was miserable and her parents were afraid she was going to do something horrible to herself if she was left to keep living the way she was. We went to a party, got drunk, and for the first time since I knocked her up, we had sex again. It wasn't great, and I continued to fuck around, not thinking that I was the reason sex with her wasn't any good. She had no clue what she was doing, and I just got in, got off, then I left her hanging and hating sex even more. It hadn't been anything more than a chore for her considering I don't think she ever got off."

He shook off the rest of his story and waved it away like the bad memory it probably was for him. "I thought that by taking care of my needs somewhere else I was sparing her. She didn't seem to enjoy sex, so I got it elsewhere. I never let her see. I thought I was granting her that much, but she told me years later that her heart used to break because I would come home smelling like them. Fucking whores and their perfumes. It never occurred to me. Then there were the times I wasn't careful enough about where lipstick marks got left behind." I blanched at his admission, knowing the state my dick had been in this morning. That statement hit a little too close to home, though I

67

didn't think Merc knew about that part of my shameful behavior - yet.

"She heard whispers from people too, probably the same club whores I'd been fucking. We had some nasty, mean bitches in here over the years. It honestly wouldn't surprise me to know they tracked her down outside of the club and gave her play-by-plays. My point is that I was an asshole who needed to grow the fuck up. Even still — I never put it in her face the way you did with that girl last night."

I hung my head, ashamed of myself. He was right. Deck was right. I'd done far worse to Anna than she deserved. In the big scheme of things her fuck up was looking like an explainable blip while mine would probably prove devastating to any future we could have had, even as friends raising a kid together. Finally, I glanced up to him with pleading eyes. "Is she okay?"

"She's safe, but no, she's not okay. That girl is in a world of pain and she doesn't even blame you. Which is what makes the whole thing complete shit, by the way. She blames herself in some crazy 'original sin' theory. She screwed up, so everything bad that follows is essentially her fault in her eyes."

"Fuck!" I hissed out

Merc started messaging someone with his phone for a few minutes before glancing back over at me. "You gonna set her up at your place?" I nodded. That was the plan all along, if only I hadn't stupidly stopped in the clubhouse to try to clear my warped brain from the layers of cobwebs. I just hadn't been able to see my situation for what it had been instead of what I'd made it out to be.

"You have a room to use here if you need it, but I gotta tell you... If you want any kind of relationship with her, not coming home at night shouldn't be an option you choose after what she saw last night."

"I won't be staying here unless she wants me to," I informed him.

"My advice?" I nodded, giving him the go-ahead to continue with it. "Even if she wants you to, stay at home, on the couch if you need to. She might not see the gesture for what it is right away, but eventually she will and that beats the shit out of how she'll feel alternatively if she has to wonder what you're up to while staying here."

"Assuming she'll even care after what I've already put her through."

"She's young, pregnant, hormonal, and has had eyes for you before. She'll care," Merc assured me. At least, he tried to do so. I wasn't sure I was buying what he was selling at this point. I'd fucked up some kind of bad. I sat there absorbing everything before he finally tapped on his desk to get my attention. "Now, go get the girl and take her home."

When I arrived at Merc's house, the first thing I noticed was that the woman who captivated me all those months ago was sitting wrapped all around herself in the swing on the front porch. Her face was settled to the side resting one cheek against her knees with her arms wrapped tightly around legs that were pulled up tightly to her chest. The beat of my heart stuttered at seeing her like that. Part of me was in awe of her beauty once again. Another felt the hot flush of shame wash over me as it occurred to me that she may be tucked into herself because of all the shit I'd put her through in the past 24 hours. She didn't even wait for me to put the truck in park in order to get out and help her into my truck. She simply got up from her spot on the porch swing and walked to the passenger side of the truck, hauled her butt inside, put on her seatbelt, was reaching for the door about the same time I came out of my stupor..

I had been standing there, just outside the driver's side door of my truck, stunned stupid for a minute as I tried to figure out how to best approach this situation. "I'm sorry, I would have helped," I started to say. I didn't get the rest out though because she shut the door, barely giving me time to dodge out of the way before metal clicked metal and shut her away from me. Hell, she just missed slamming my fingers inside. Pissed. She was definitely pissed. Rightfully so, but I honestly wasn't sure what to do with a pissed off and pregnant woman. To be safe, I did nothing except hop into the truck and drive. I backed us out of Merc's driveway, taking note that Tiger Lily was scowling my way from the porch steps.

Once we were on the road, the only noise was the sound of the engine and any other vehicles around us. Anna hadn't even bothered to look over to my side of the truck once. Her eyes were glued to whatever she was looking at directly in front of her. She failed to move for so long, I worried maybe she'd become catatonic or something. Did women just hysterically go catatonic when they grew too upset with a man? Fuck if I knew how they worked.

When we stopped at a light, I took a chance and glanced over at her. She didn't seem angry, she just looked to be resigned and sad. She must have noticed me watching her, and for the first time since she shut the door of the truck, she moved. Of course, in doing so, she turned to look out the window beside her instead of straight ahead so I could no longer see her face.

As I took off from the stoplight, I glanced back over at her one more time. "Anna, I wanted to tell you how sorry I am for the way I behaved yesterday. It wasn't fair to you and you damn sure didn't deserve it. I promise, nothing like that will ever happen again."

She didn't respond, not even to flinch. I wondered if I had

broken her. I decided it was best to wait until we got home to attempt any further groveling. At least that way, the rest of world wouldn't have a front row seat to seeing me beg her forgiveness and how fast she was going to shoot it down. I knew at this point, I didn't deserve it at all. I wouldn't give it if the shoe was on the other foot. I'd already proven that much.

Chapter 6

APOLOGIES

ANNA

He apologized. There was really no telling what the apology

was actually for since there were so many things I felt he did

wrong yesterday. Maybe it was for my ruined wedding? Probably

not. Someone most likely told him that I saw his make-out

session with another woman, or about all the other women who

were hanging on him. Then again, maybe the apology was for

leaving me stranded while he got drunk at the club in the first place. I wasn't even sure he would feel bad at all about the blow job he got since he looked as though he enjoyed it a whole heck of a lot. Besides, it was doubtful that he knew someone had told me about that. No matter which part he was apologizing for I was actually just shocked that he'd done it at all.

Despite my shock, I refused to acknowledge him while we were still in his truck. I didn't want to upset him and then be stranded somewhere else for who knew how long. I wouldn't put it past the asshole to leave me on the side of the road somewhere. I'm sure the brothers would believe him if he simply said we stopped to get gas and I ran off. I was the liar in this relationship after all.

I had never been to Joker's house so I was a little surprised when we pulled up to a small two-bedroom ranch-style house with a carport off of one end. The house was probably no more than a thousand square feet, and certainly didn't compare to the one I had grown up in with its four bedrooms and multiple-car attached garage. I didn't need all that, but still I wondered about why he had chosen this place. I actually wished I could ask how long he'd had the house. Did he buy it when he left the military? There were so many questions I would have asked if we were the people who had gotten along so famously before my lies caught up to me. Back when he was a prospect named Evan Masters and I was just a girl named Lise. He would have answered my thousand and one questions brightly.

THE PRINCESS *and the* PROSPECT

Now, I didn't think I'd get more than a grunt or a one word answer telling me it really wasn't my business because our marriage was for medical coverage until the baby was born only. I glanced around the property as I held my tongue. While the house was on the smaller side, the yard was overly large with plenty of room for him to expand when he finally got the family he really wanted one day. The yard was surrounded by a thick line, or maybe it was multiple rows, of trees down three of the four sides making it feel very isolated from anyone else in the area. The Spanish moss hanging from the limbs in the trees added to an otherworldly spooky quality that was sure to be worse as night fell.

Honestly, I wasn't certain if I'd like living here or not. On the one hand, it looked cozy. On the other, it already felt a bit like my own personal prison, especially considering I no longer had a car of my own and his house wasn't close to town.

My tummy did flips at that thought. It was just now hitting me that I was married to man who hated me, and I was having his baby, and had to live with him. If only he had been the Evan Masters I first met. I would have done cartwheels in the front yard to have been moving in with him. The man that sat beside me watching me take everything in was cold, mean, and heartless. He was the man who cheated on me on our wedding night. Worry finally settled deep into my bones. Would anyone know if he was mistreating me out here all by ourselves? Would

I be safe? Would he force me to perform my wifely duties? Would I get any choices from here on out? My heart started beating wildly in my chest as the panic set in. I couldn't breathe. I just couldn't catch my… Oh God!

"Anna? Jesus, Anna take a deep breath for me," he called out as he pushed my body forward, putting my head between my knees. Now, blow it out. Easy. That's it. Deep breath in, again." He coached me through getting my breathing back under control. I refused to look at him after that. I also noticed he was rubbing small circles on my back in an effort to help calm me.

"What was that all about?" He finally asked once I had everything back under control.

"I don't want to be raped," I cried and then continued to word vomit. "Is it even rape since we're married? I have a baby to think about. I can't get diseases you might be carrying now. This place looks like a prison. Everything's closing in and I… I… Oh God!"

"What the fuck?" He spat out and I hesitantly glanced over at Joker who had stopped rubbing circles on my back. He was no longer touching me at all and had his hands up in the air near his shoulders. The look on his face, he seemed absolutely horrified. "Christ Anna. I would never force you or hurt you in any way."

"You already hurt me, and how should I know? You're a stranger to me. I never would have thought you'd be so cruel to anyone, but now I know better."

He moved quickly then and started peeling a key off of his keyring. He laid it on the seat beside me. "There, go in, make yourself at home. I'll go back to the clubhouse since you think you have to worry I'd rape you!"

To my surprise, he didn't sound angry. He just sounded hurt. I couldn't help how my anxiety and thoughts spiraled though. This was a horrible position to be in and right in that moment I hated everyone and had no one. My family all let this happen. I wished Toby were still here. He would have never allowed this. He knew. I'd confided in my big brother before he got killed. I told him about my crush on Deck's friend. He'd asked me to wait until I was old enough.

I couldn't stand the thought of watching Joker get with other women, but I'd agreed. Then Toby was killed and we found out about Gretchen and how she was going to have a baby, but she lost it. I understood then that life was short and you had to take what you wanted. I never wanted it like this though. Toby had been right. He would be so upset with me now, but never would he have just handed me over to a stranger the way everyone else seemed to have done. Even knowing this had been my choice, Toby would have found a way to talk me out of it.

I got out of the truck making sure to take my bag with me and once I was on the covered front stoop Joker backed his truck up and drove away. He didn't' even stay to see me safely inside or show me around. It wasn't like I could help the panic attack I'd had. Once I made my way inside I realized I was already standing in the living room area and there was an open floor plan that led to the kitchen as well. He had furniture, sparse though it may have been. There was a brown leather couch and reclining chair along with a smaller loveseat. The kitchen had a little dining area built in where a table and four chairs sat. They were all also a deep cherry wood brown, as if the house was afraid of color. I nearly stumbled on the large suitcases by the door. They were mine, and I wondered briefly when they had been deposited there. It also made me curious as to whether I would have a room here or if I was meant to sleep on the couch or something.

It would suck to have to live out of suitcases until after the baby was born, but I figured I could manage. As I moved to the only hallway off of the left side of the living room I saw there was a full bath with sink, toilet, and shower/tub combo at the end of the hallway. Off to the right was a door that led to a bedroom that was pretty no-frills. It had a utilitarian full size bed, a small chair, one bed-side table, and a six drawer dresser that stood nearly waist high for me. In other words, like the house, it was on the smaller side.

Looking left the door was open there too. I walked into what must have been the master bedroom. A king size bed, which had been made up nicely, multiple dressers, and a television on top of the one facing the bed took up most of the space. There were three doors on the wall facing back toward where the bathroom would be if I were still out in the hall. On the far left was a closet that was mostly empty with the exception of two boxes on a high shelf. On the right was a similar walk-in closet which was full of all of Joker's things. I backed out quickly as soon as I realized that.

The middle door led to a gorgeous bathroom with a garden tub separate shower and toilet area and then his and hers sinks. There were mirrors up behind both the sinks and then all along the wall behind the tub. I stared at myself in those mirrors for a few minutes seeing a girl who looked far too tired and far too fun down to just be 17-years-old. I didn't want to acknowledge my lack of sleep or care for myself over the past two days. If I did, I'd have to face the fact that I was already a crappy mother.

I couldn't remember the last time I'd eaten. I moved to the kitchen to see if he had anything I could grab quickly, but there was nothing. He had a box of Captain Crunch cereal in a cabinet, some condiments and beer in the fridge and not much else beyond water straight from the tap. I found the glasses and grabbed some water to take with me to the smaller bedroom. There I sat gingerly on the bed and sipped my water as I took in the room. There was enough space here for a crib and maybe a small changing table if I organized things carefully. The chair would probably be a good choice for sitting in while nursing the baby.

It took me a minute to realize that by the time the baby was out of me and the six weeks post-partum checkup was done I would probably have to move into a place of my own. That meant I needed to find a job as soon as possible so I could save up some money in advance.

Once I was finished with my water I stood and put down my canvas satchel I'd brought in from Joker's truck, thankful it had still been there after I'd left it in his truck the other night. I moved to the living room and worked hard to drag each of the heavy suitcases back to the bedroom where I could go through them and see what all had been packed up for me. My mother had told me not to worry that she would see to it, and make sure my things got settled in that way I could be stress free after the wedding. Little did she know… There was no such thing as stress free in my life anymore.

My stomach growled again warning me that I needed to eat very soon or I would start feeling sick again. I'd had enough of morning sickness that lasted throughout the day before. I didn't want to start having that again. Remembering that there wasn't any food in the house though, I just grabbed another glass of water and made an internal to-do list. I needed to be able to go grocery shopping at some point. I assumed I'd have to break down and call my sister in the morning to ask her to take me since I didn't have a lot of money. I couldn't afford to waste any of it on taxi fare.

I got up and closed the door to the bedroom noting that there wasn't a lock on the door, much to my dismay. Then I laid down on the too-soft bed and cried until sleep finally claimed my weary body.

I turned the corner, laughing with abandon as I tried to use the doorjamb to slow my progress before I slipped and fell. It gave him just enough time to spring at me. He wrapped his arms around my waist and lifted me up off of my feet with my back to his front. Giggles spilled out of my mouth as the happiness I felt in the moment filled me to bursting and it was the only way to not just burst apart and float away with the clouds.

"I got you," he whispered into my ear, breathing heavily as he did. His warm breath on my skin sent a shiver of anticipation through my body. Never had my body experienced need in this way before. Every piece of me being felt electrified as his lips found the shell of my ear and nibbled there.

"What do you plan to do with me now?" My voice was raw and breathy all at the same time, sounding completely foreign to me, but apparently he liked it.

He growled low in his throat as if my question tortured him. Then he answered and everything in my lower region pulled taut in response. "Oh, I think you know," he answered before tossing me on his bed. I bounced, forcing more laughter from me before he pounced and proceeded to attack my body with gentle nibbles from his teeth. When he managed to snag one of my nipples through the thin material of the tank top I wore, he bit down a little harder causing me to squirm and moan out in response.

"That's it, beautiful, so responsive for me all the time."

"Evan," I cried out his name when he treated my other nipple to the same attention. "Please," I begged.

"Please, what Lise?" I jerked back from him at the name he used. Even though it was all he ever called me, besides beautiful, it always felt wrong to hear it. He should be calling me Anna by now. Especially since we had moved on to being intimate with one another. Evan worked to get the tank top up and off my body, which thankfully concealed my reaction. Then he bit, sucked, and licked down my torso before relieving me of the pastel floral skirt and ivory, silk panties I had worn that day.

"Love that you always look so put together with that librarian vibe and then you come apart so hot under my hands, my tongue, my cock," he told me as he continued to worship every part of me. Down one leg and up the other after a playful kiss was placed on each of my toes, then when he came back to the apex of my thighs he dipped his head in and swiped his tongue up my seam.

"Oh, God, Evan!" I cried out feeling the warmth and the slick wetness that was left behind each time he dipped his tongue

into my most sensitive parts. I reached out and took hold of the longer strands of hair on the top of his head and guided him where I needed him most. I felt, more than heard, the chuckle he let out as a result. He always thought it was funny when his innocent little Lise tried to take charge.

He reached up and grabbed hold of my hands, bringing them firmly down to my sides as he held onto them to ensure I wouldn't try to take over again. "We have all night, Lise," he told me before slowly licking me from back to front again. We didn't have all night. I had to get home at some point in case anyone decided to be a good parent and check that I was actually where I was supposed to be. I wasn't sure how many more nights the rolled up pillows and blankets would fool my parents. Besides, we were running a huge risk being here together at the clubhouse. I supposed I was the one really running the risk since Evan was still unaware how dangerous us being together actually was.

The guilt I felt about having still not told him the truth nearly pulled me from the erotic pleasure I was receiving. Nearly, but nothing could compete with Evan and his magic tongue. Well, nothing beyond that moment when he moved up my body and sank himself deep inside of me.

"Couldn't wait, beautiful. You've been driving me mad all day in that little skirt of yours. I needed…" he hesitated as he thrust into me again, and then pulled out at a leisurely pace, *taking his time to savor the feel of my slick folds wrapped around him. Now that he was no longer holding my hands down I moved them to run my nails gently up and down his back. It gave him pause, as it always did. He enjoyed the dual sensation of being sunk deep inside me as I brought gooseflesh to his skin with each stroke back and forth of my nails. When I was ready for him to really fuck me I simply increased the pressure of my nails in his back and it was like pushing a button that unleashed his passionate fury on me.*

His pace picked up, our sweat-slickened skin slapping together, grunts and moans, mixing to become the music of our love making.

"You have to do better," a strange voice called out. I glanced around, but there was no one here beyond Evan and myself. He seemed oblivious to the voice I had just heard.

"I realize that," Evan told me as he thrust harder into me.

"What?" I asked as the room around us began to fade into a foggy gray nothing.

"Why weren't you here with her?" I glanced around again trying to find the disembodied voice in the ever thickening fog.

"She didn't want me," Evan told me – no he told the voice – as his green eyes drifted further from me, the heat of his body no longer warming my own. The cold, reality that came crashing in mad me very aware my dream was at an end.

Being jostled from sleep by strange voices when I didn't

recognize my surroundings was disconcerting at best. Still, I managed to keep calm enough to not move or give away the fact that I was now awake. The room would have been dark, extremely dark, making me think I'd been asleep a good while. The problem with my theory being that there was light shining in from near the doorway. As I glanced around the opposite side of the room from the door – the way I had been facing while asleep – I noticed the sparse furnishings and the past two days came screaming back to me in a clarity that I didn't want to acknowledge.

"You have some explaining to do," a familiar feminine voice whisper-hissed. Only the hissing part was too loud to contain the whisper she was trying for. "Why is my sister in there? And why do you have no food in this house? You realize she's growing a baby – your baby – don't you?" What in the world was Ever doing here? I assumed she was angrily speaking to Joker at that point since there was no way the baby I carried belonged to anyone else.

"I forgot I'd need to get food in here. I've had a lot going on too, you know? And I didn't chose the room for her. I guess she did."

"So you just happened to toss her bags in here and you didn't think she'd take that hint?" Ever asked him. I felt my face flush knowing he hadn't done that. I had.

"The bags were out by the door last time I was here," he

admitted.

Ever gasped. "Those were heavy, extremely so. She shouldn't have been moving them! Where were you when she did that?"

"The clubhouse," he answered her, the attitude evident in his voice as he did so. "I just dropped her off to give her space to settle in earlier."

"You dropped her off? Like you didn't even come inside to make sure she was okay being here, show her around, or make sure she had everything she needed before you left?"

"It's a small house. Besides, she had a goddamn panic attack on the way here and called this place a prison before she basically begged me not to rape her and give her diseases. I didn't think it was wise to stick around out here alone with her under the circumstances."

"Oh, my poor baby," Ever sighed. "We all thought she'd be okay. That this is what she'd want." I heard a smack. "Then you had to go and be a complete asshole to her. No wonder she had a panic attack. New husband is a jerk, new house out in the middle of nowhere, no food, baby on the way, and you behaving the way you did at your wedding and afterward. Jesus. I can't allow this to keep happening to her. She doesn't deserve this."

"I fucking get it!" He roared the words at my sister. "I'm fucking up. I know this, but I don't know how to fix what's already been done."

"You don't get it because it's not about you. It's about that girl in there who had her entire life shifted completely off its axis."

I heard his frustrated huff before he answered her. "And I didn't?"

"Do you still live in your own house? Drive your own bike? Truck? Have your own money? You hold the same job, right? You have your club to go to when you need to blow off some steam, hang with people who like you, yeah? My sister has none of those securities you have. She has nothing that is the same in her life right now. She's in a new house, not attending school, has no job, and nothing to call her own except her clothing and journals. That's it. Her friends all thought she was weird for getting married and dropping out so they aren't even talking to her right now."

There was a moment when everything got quiet and then Ever spoke again. "Most importantly though... Are you growing a baby in your belly that is fucking with your body from the inside out? She is and she's doing it all while not even having anything in her life that she's comfortable with right now. So cry me a river when you tell me shit is changed for you too, but I don't see how it's come close to what my sister is facing right now. Maybe think about that the next time you get the desire to act like an asshole."

It was quiet again for a moment before I heard my sister's

voice again. This time it came from a little further away. "I'll come get her and her things in the morning. She can stay with Deck and me."

"What? No! Why would you suggest that?"

"Because you're both obviously miserable. Besides, I know what you did last night and when she finds out – if she doesn't already know – she won't stay with you anyway."

"She doesn't know and it would only hurt her at this point. I know I fucked up. I fucked up the whole goddamn day because I was lost in my own anger. I really liked her before. Hell, I was falling in love with her," he admitted to my sister something he'd never bothered admitting to me. "I was devastated when I thought all of it was a lie. I get it now. That doesn't change how I let my anger fuel me and my decisions though. That's my regret to live with."

"The problem is that you might have regrets for your behavior, but my sister now has to live with those memories."

"Come on, please, let's go in the other room before we wake her. She needs her sleep."

"Fine. I'm still coming back in the morning and if she wants to leave, I'm taking her."

"I won't hold her hostage. No matter how she felt when she saw the place, my house won't be a prison for her." That was the last I heard as my door was shut and they continued to move away from it.

Chapter 7

HIDING

The chair in my living room had never felt uncomfortable

before. Sitting in it so long while waiting for Anna to surface from the bedroom was beginning to make me rethink my original opinion of the furniture. Then again, I supposed there wasn't a piece on the planet comfortable enough to withstand such a long wait. She had to come out of that room eventually, right? Worry started to set in about an hour ago. I'd debated whether or not I should just go check on her, but after her panic attack the day before I wasn't sure if that would make matters worse. I'd never been so insecure with myself or my decisions as I felt now. The worst part was that I knew I had brought all of this on myself.

After arguing with Ever last night about her coming to get Anna this morning, I'd gone out and bought groceries for the house before returning and sitting vigil in the damn chair that now had me feeling stiff all over. I felt horrible when Ever pointed out the fact that I'd left a pregnant woman in the house with no food to eat, and then I hadn't bothered to show again for hours. Hell, I had just made it back to the house, thinking I could sneak in and just sleep on the couch, when Ever showed up to check on her sister since no one had heard from her all day.

I was about to stand and stretch, resigning myself to the fact that I would have to go check on Anna, and just deal with the fall out. I couldn't stand it if I waited much longer, only to find out she'd had something go wrong with the pregnancy and no one checked on her. It was one of my biggest fears after I watched a few videos about nightmare pregnancies. Fuck! I don't know why I ever did that. The images that were burned in my brain had been haunting my dreams ever since, only the face always changed to Anna's instead of the women who had been in the videos – some of which didn't make it in the end.

Before I could move, the bedroom door finally opened and Anna stepped out of the room. She stiffened a moment, as if preparing for a fight, then without looking my way, she darted into the bathroom like a frightened mouse trying to scurry around unseen. Something about that broke my heart a little bit more.

Not for the first time, I wondered what Double-D had been thinking when he strongly suggested this for us. I wasn't sure if it was something he had actually forced on her. It wasn't exactly done that way with me. I had been given a choice, and I accepted this marriage as a way to make sure my child was taken care of. I hated to admit that I also did so I could get dirt on the girl in case we had to fight for the kid later. After learning some things, and opening my eyes to the situation a bit more, I felt shame wash through me in the face of my ulterior motives. Still, just because I had agreed to this situation, that didn't mean Double-D had given Anna the same leeway.

I sat contemplating that and going over the words in my head to relinquish her from the commitment she'd made in such a way that Double-D would never know. I wouldn't be the one to hold her prisoner to this life if she hadn't chosen it of her own free will. Another douchebag move I'd made was in not checking with her first if she really wanted this.

The bathroom was the door at the end of the hall so when Anna came back out she had no choice but to see me seated in the chair drinking my third damn cup of Joe. When it appeared she was just going to run back to her room, I called out to her, halting her in her tracks.

"Anna!" Her eyes finally came up to meet mine as her shoulders slumped in defeat momentarily. Then she squared them off and made her way to the living room with her head held high. "Can you sit so we can talk? It's important." I glanced at my phone. We had about 45 minutes before Ever was supposed to show up and whisk her sister away from me.

She sat perched on the edge of the couch looking ready to bolt at any moment, though her hands were demurely folded in her lap giving the momentary illusion that she wasn't going to flee.

"Anna, I know I've handled most of this poorly. You don't know how sorry I am about that. I was caught off guard yesterday when you thought I might force you…"

"I don't think that." She told me in a small voice that was so unlike her, it was startling. "It was just me babbling all the fleeting thoughts I had during my freak out."

"Regardless, hearing you say that in the middle of freaking out caught me off guard and I didn't handle it the right way. I was afraid to be alone in the house with you, so I left to give you time to settle in. I didn't mean to leave you stranded here though. For that, I'm sorry."

"Okay." She offered the one word response with a shrug of her shoulders. The quiet stretched out between us for a moment before I carried on, since she didn't seem to have anything else to say.

"I also didn't mean for you to take the guest room. I thought we could turn it into a nursery together." I started to tell her my plan, but her face drained of color when I said that.

"I don't want to sleep with you," she blurted out.

"What? I never said that we would be sleeping together."

She shook her head adamantly. "There's only one other bedroom in this house," she confirmed. Then her eyes widened. "Sorry, I didn't think." She squirmed on the leather sofa. "This will do," she said as she patted the couch. "I just need to know where I can put my stuff so it's out of the way."

It took me a minute to grasp what she was saying. She thought I wasn't even going to give her the comfort of her own space, or even a bed, when she was pregnant? What kind of a royal asshole had I been that she would think so poorly of me?

"Anna, I meant for you to take the master. You're pregnant. I figured being closer to the bathroom would be a good thing; and I can take the couch."

"But all of your stuff is in there. It's your house."

"Did you look around yesterday?" She nodded her head. "Come here a minute," I demanded as I stood from the chair I'd been sitting in and moved to the master bedroom with her following behind me reluctantly. "Look, I made the bed with fresh linens and blankets for you," I told her as I moved to the left closet door. "This is completely empty for all your stuff.

There are dressers in here so you can keep all of your things completely separate from mine if that's what you want." I sighed when I saw her eye my closet. "If I had a garage I could move my stuff into I would. It'll just have to do for now. I planned to sleep in the spare room until we start working on the nursery, then the couch will be fine."

"How was I supposed to know that?"

"Well, I was meant to be here, giving you a tour of my vast estate," I joked to lighten the mood. "Then I had my own freak out when you thought I might be capable of raping you."

"Sorry," she apologized.

"Don't. You're allowed to feel what you feel, Anna. It's not like anyone has made this easy on you. I still don't know why your parents pushed you into doing this."

"They didn't," she informed me.

"I thought…"

"My dad made threats about a shotgun wedding to punish you. Neither of my parents expected me to follow through with it." Something in her eyes told me that there was more to what she was saying. They might not have expected her to follow through, but she didn't really expect them to allow it to happen either. They had. I wondered how she truly felt about that now. Still, I was floored by her admission.

"Why did you agree to do it then?"

She placed her hand over her belly. "This is my burden, not

theirs. I didn't want to live in their house, expecting my parents to help raise my baby. They're ready to retire soon and they've always talked about all the traveling they would do once the kids were grown. Me having a baby in their house would have derailed their plans."

"So you chose to marry me and live here – not knowing what to expect – so that your pregnancy didn't disrupt your parents' retirement?"

"Yes," she answered without any hesitation.

Merc's words during our conversation yesterday came back to me full force. The meaning behind them suddenly very clear. *"That girl has always been selfless. She just wants to make other people smile."* I was contemplating that, and had remained quiet so Anna spoke up again. The nervousness in her voice as she did so was evident.

"It's your baby too so I didn't think it would be a problem for you. You'd have access to the baby and you have the clubhouse so you can get away from me and do whatever you need to." I didn't miss the dejected tone her words had devolved to at the end of that statement. She imagined every time I went to the clubhouse, it was to get my dick wet in some way. That made me both hate myself, because I knew my own actions had helped enforce her belief, and angry because that wasn't something I would normally ever consider doing once married or in a serious relationship. The fact that she hadn't even used an accusatory tone, and instead had been saddened by her own words, but equally resigned to them, caused an ache to form in my stomach. Actually, it was closer to my chest. I had done that to her. I'd made her feel that way, and the regret I already felt re-doubled.

"Anna, about what you saw that night. I was angry and hadn't thought everything through yet. I let my anger fuel my drinking and then that killed my judgement. It should have never happened. It will never happen again. I promise." Her only response was a negligible motion of her shoulders rising and falling in a half-assed version of a shrug. I didn't get to soothe whatever feelings my words caused that she was trying to hide from me because a knock on the door stopped me short.

When I got up to open the door, Ever was standing there with Deck, both demanding to speak to Anna. I opened the door wider so they could both come in. Ever moved quickly to sit beside her sister, whispering in hushed tones as Deck moved inside the door and stood there looking over the place with a critical eye.

"No," Anna was saying to Ever while shaking her head back and forth as I sat down in the chair once more. I really wished things were different and I was sitting on the couch with Anna in my lap instead of feeling as though this huge wall stood between us and it was made of some pretty impenetrable stuff.

"Anna, you can't stay here," Ever told her quietly while

glaring over Anna's shoulder toward me.

"Why on Earth not?"

"You're obviously not comfortable here," her sister answered back.

Anna simply shrugged. "I'm not going with you, but I do have a favor to ask."

"What?"

"Could you give me a ride to town?"

"Why don't I just take you to go get your car? I'm sure that dad wouldn't want you to go without it considering you're living all the way out here."

Anna gave Ever an odd look before answering. "Daddy didn't take my car from me. He would never do that," she told Ever assuredly. Ever just gave her a dubious look right back, obviously not feeling the same trust in their father that Anna did.

"Then why don't you have your car here with you?"

"I sold it," Anna stated simply.

"What? Why in the world would you sell your car? You obviously need it!"

"I didn't have any money. Now, I have a little set aside for the baby's stuff," she admitted. Her cheeks pinked up, showing the embarrassment she clearly felt about having to sell her car to afford things for our baby. I just sat there, mouth agape for a minute, trying to wrap my head around the fact that I had been such a fucking shit that this girl thought she needed to sell her only real possession in order to help care for our child. Fuck my life. She was going to break me. More to the point, my own stupid actions were doing enough of a number on her that her reactions to it were breaking me.

"You don't have to pay for any of the baby's stuff, Anna. I have it all covered," I informed her as well as Ever and Deck who were both staring at me with hate-filled eyes.

"No, I do. I'm already a burden. I need…"

"You are not a goddamn burden!" I snapped. Judging by her flinch I'd said it a little too loudly, or maybe too passionately. "You can use the truck until we can get you another car. I have the bike so it's no problem for you to use it."

"No really," Anna turned pleading eyes to her sister.

"I'll have appointments at odd hours with work, Anna. Using his truck sounds like your best option for now."

Anna's answer came to her sister in a small voice, "Okay."

"Now, do you need Deck to grab your things so you can come stay with us?" Ever asked her, obviously feeling as though her little sister was acquiescing to everything. Once again Anna shook her head in the negative.

"Anna, if you're uncomfortable here, you don't have to stay. We don't mind you being at our house. It's huge."

"No!" Anna's statement was firm. "I'm pregnant, Ever."

"I know. That's part of why I'm offering."

Anna huffed out a breath of frustration as she made eye contact with her sister. "Y'all are working on the house. None of the extra rooms are fully done yet and it's probably not good for me to be around all the construction stuff."

"Shit!" Ever hissed. Once again, Anna proved she had truly thought about everyone else, and pretty much every alternative scenario they might come up with.

"You could go back home. Momma-Luce didn't want you moving here anyway."

"No," Anna stated adamantly.

"But," Ever started to argue when Deck finally interceded.

"Babe, why don't we leave them to it? Anna has our numbers. She can call us any time. And Anna, I finished one of the rooms last week, just in case. It's yours if you need it, or even if you simply want it." He smiled over at her before he tacked on a final hit to me. "That goes for if it's just a night, or if you need to move in for good or until you can get yourself sorted out with your own place, okay?"

"Thanks, Deck." Anna moved from where she had been sitting cockeyed on the couch facing her sister to stand and go give the man, who used to be my best friend, a hug. I hated to admit it, and wouldn't do so out loud, but I was jealous as fuck of my club brother in that moment. I hadn't touched or been touched by Anna in any way since her secret came out. It also looked like it would probably never happen again and that was all my fault. She had even puckered up at the "you may kiss the bride" part of our nuptials and I'd callously declared, "it isn't necessary," before stepping away from her. I don't know what kind of asshole monster took me over that day, but I'd have to spend the rest of my life making it up to Anna. Hell, I'd probably spend most of that time just praying she'd let me try to make it up to her.

I watched as Anna pulled back from Deck and moved to her sister, who had also stood from where she'd been perched on the couch. The two sisters hugged and as they broke the connection, Ever slid her hand into Anna's and pulled her off down the hall so they could speak in private.

"How are you doing with all of this?" Deck asked, pulling my attention away from the two women.

"You mean when I'm not completely fucking it all up?" I asked.

He grinned at me. "At least you're starting to see the error of your ways."

"Yeah, but I think my dawning realization probably came too late. She's only staying because it burdens other people the least."

Deck continued to grin at me. "I know. We all know that. Anna operates that way. I'm thinking maybe you should be smart enough to take advantage of that situation, and use the time you have with her to build a friendship, trust, or whatever else you can manage before the baby comes along."

Instead of filling me with the hope I was sure he meant to instill, I felt the dread of a deadline hanging over my head. What if I wasn't able to earn her trust before then? Would she take the baby from me? Would they let her – or help her – to disappear? I didn't think so considering what happened with Double-D and Lucy all those years ago that resulted in the possibility of Ever existing. I'm sure they didn't regret having Ever in their lives now, but I imagine they all would have given just about anything – outside of their daughter – to have the time and memories that were stolen from them when Lucy's family hid her away from Double-D while she was pregnant with Toby.

I was pretty sure that looking back on all he missed with the son that was no longer here on Earth with them was the reason Double-D had pushed so hard for the two of us to have to stick things out together for a while. He was hoping that another family wouldn't have to go through what they did, especially since it was his own daughter and grandchild involved.

Chapter 8

ANNA

What in the world had I managed to get myself into? That question repeated in my head darn near hourly. I didn't think there was a right answer to the question though. I could see that Joker felt bad about what he'd done, or how he'd treated me, but that didn't take away having to live through those things. On the flip side, I was daunted by my family wanting me to move in with them. I had my own plan, but I didn't want to tell anyone about it because I didn't want to jinx myself. What if I failed? I had already failed everyone who thought I was a good girl. I couldn't bear the disappointed looks from everyone again.

The real reason I was waiting for my sister to give me a ride into town was so that I could get a job and make some money. I just didn't need my family breathing down my neck about it. I knew everyone involved would attempt to open their pockets or buy me what they thought I needed. That wasn't what I wanted. I figured if I was adult enough to be bringing a child into this world, I should be adult enough to take responsibility for the financial aspects of having that child.

Besides, there was only so long I could stay shacked up here with Joker. Eventually, he would want to bring his women around so he could get laid. Being at the clubhouse was out of the question for him in a few ways since my father, Merc, and Deck would be there to see what he was up to. No matter how much I wished I could make myself indifferent to the idea of it, I couldn't. It would kill me every time. It was going to absolutely slay me one day when he would get serious with a woman and bring them around our child. There's no way I could deal with watching the man I thought I'd been in love with play house with our child and some other woman.

So, that brought me back to the issue at hand. I needed to get a job so that I could save up money for a place to live with my baby. At least then, I wouldn't have to witness first hand when Joker had a woman over with him, or worse, near our child.

"Hey Anna Banana," Ever called out when she pulled up to ride me into town.

"Hi Ever. Thanks for doing this."

"You don't have to thank me for being a big sister and making sure you have a ride."

"Yes, I do," I insisted.

"Anna?" My name was a question on her lips. "Are you sure about all of this?"

"I'm sure," I explained again, for what felt like the tenth time.

"I liked Joker. I thought he was a great guy, but what I saw after your split from him, when you told him about the baby. The way he reacted since then…" she licked her lips and side-eyed me as she drove. It was clear she was trying to go easy with what she wanted to point out. I nearly laughed, because there was no need to go easy about things I'd already experienced for myself first hand. "Honey, he's been a dick. Your wedding night," she started to tell me something. I was sure she probably was going to shed light on the situation I already knew about, and I didn't want to talk about it with her.

"Ever," I called out to stop her. "I already know all these things. I know them, and I still think this is for the best," I hesitated before I tacked on two last words. "For now."

She offered up a quick smile and then turned her entire focus back to her driving. "If you say so, but I want you to know I'm here for you. Don't feel like you're trapped in this situation. If things get bad…" She stopped and then started again. "I don't want things to get bad for you. So if anything happens that makes you any more uncomfortable then you've already been made, please, promise me that you will come stay with us until you can figure out what you want to do for your future. We'll help you reach your goals. You don't have to do it on your own."

"You did," I argued with her.

She grinned. "I did because I wasn't pregnant, but I am stupidly stubborn."

"That must come from our dad then, because we have that in common," I told her and we both chuckled a bit then. It felt great to be able to smile and laugh again for a minute.

"Do you need me to stay with you, or did you just want me to drop you off somewhere specific?" Ever finally asked me.

"I just need you to drop me at the library. I have some studying to do and research for a paper I'm going to have to turn in. I'll probably need to get dropped off a couple days this week if you don't mind."

"I don't mind. Just text me when you're done and either Deck or me will come take you back home."

"Thank you."

Once Ever dropped me off at the library, I went inside to check the help wanted pages from the local paper, along with doing an online search for jobs in the area. Most of them were the typical teenage jobs working fast food. I applied to all the ones I could online. Then I went to a couple that were within walking distance of the library because they required that people apply in person. By the fourth rejection, I was feeling daunted. I wondered what it was about me that had people shuffling me out the door so quickly, but honestly it probably just had to do with my lack of experience at pretty much anything.

Three days in a row I walked around different areas of downtown looking for work. Either they weren't hiring, had already hired someone, or just plain told me no and then stared at the slight baby bump I had showing that meant I either drank too much beer as a teenager, or I was baking a bun in my oven. I rolled my eyes at the thought. Like pregnant women didn't need to work more than most people. We had another person built in that was counting on us.

I was nearly ready to give up, admit defeat, and take my mom up on her offer to see me through college before I venture out on my own with the baby, when I saw another help wanted sign in a window. When I glanced up, my eyes brightened and hope filled my chest, even though I knew it was a long shot. It would be the best job in the world for me. I walked inside smiling at the tinkling bell that rained music down on me as I stepped inside. "Hi, we'll be right with you," a disembodied voice called out from somewhere around a curtained off area. It didn't take long until a frazzled woman with medium-length white blond hair backed out of the curtain holding boxes stacked so high I couldn't get a good look at her face.

"Do you need help with that?" I asked in a hushed tone as not to startle her.

"No, I got it. Just," she huffed as she stumbled a bit, knocking the middle box into the counter. "Give me…" she tried again as the top one almost teetered off, but not quite. "A sec," she finished as she managed to lift her burden just enough to be able to set the bottom box down on top of the counter. She patted the leaning tower of boxes gently and then walked out from behind them. Her grin fell almost immediately as she took in the sight of me standing there.

"Anna?"

"Hi, Gretchen, how are you?"

"I'm okay," she started to say before her eyes drooped down to my mid-section and I watched as they sort of bugged out, and her dimpled chin began to wobble momentarily before she got herself, and her reaction, under control. "Is that what I think it is?" She asked, pointing at my belly. I nodded slowly, not knowing how she was going to take my pregnancy news. "Oh boy, I think we have a lot to discuss then," she offered with a sweet smile before directing me over to a slouchy microfiber couch toward the opposite end of the lobby area.

"We do, because I thought you still worked at Permanent Marks with Ever," I stated as we moved to go take a seat. She immediately sat beside me and pulled one of my hands into hers, and then gave up her original intent with the simple gesture and pulled me into a tight hug instead.

"I do. This is my sister's studio. She had so much work on her books that she had to finally give in and rent studio space, plus ask for help," she indicated the help wanted sign in the window that had drawn me in.

"That's why I'm here, actually."

"I don't understand. Maybe you should back up and tell me how that happened," she said, indicating my belly. "Then you can tell me why your family is making you get a job while you are in this condition."

"It's a long story," I explained.

"I'm all ears. We aren't open until next week." She got up and quickly jogged over to the door and locked it before coming to sit with me once more. "Sorry, that should have been locked to begin with. I'm glad it wasn't in this case though."

"Me too," I agreed. Then I launched into the story of how I met Joker, what I did to screw things up, and how I was heartbroken about having done so when I finally realized I was pregnant. Then I surprised myself by telling her everything else. Absolutely everything from my horror show of wedding to the night after, and my first day in Joker's house. The subsequent days we'd spent barely talking to one another got lumped in there too, along with the fact that I knew he had to work, but that I didn't know if that was what he was actually doing with all of his time when he was away or if he was out seeing other women.

Gretchen looked steaming mad by the time I was done. "If Toby were here, he would have kicked that man's ass and strung him up by his balls until he saw the error of his ways. What the hell was your dad thinking? What are Ever and Deck thinking to keep letting you stick it out there?" She stood and started pacing. "Maybe you should take Ever up on staying with her for a while." She turned and glanced back at me. "I'd tell you to come stay with me, but I took over the apartment above Permanent Marks after Ever left, so I don't have much room."

"It's okay, Gretch."

"No, it's not. You should be overjoyed right now with the blessing you're carrying, not worried about how you're going to be able to save money for when the baby gets here." Her eyes filled with wetness that I could tell she was trying hard not to let fall. Then she sat beside me again. "Have you felt the baby move yet?"

I shook my head no. "The doctor says it should be soon though. I might be able to see the sex at my next appointment, but I don't think I want to know. I kind of want that to be a surprise, you know?"

Gretchen gave me a sad smile. "I do know. I felt the same way."

"I'm…" I started to apologize, but she stopped me with the

shake of her head and her fingers moving to rest gently on my lips.

"It's okay. I've been in therapy, honey. I'm strong enough to talk about it now, I promise. It still hurts, every day. Between Toby and the baby, I lost a lot that day. It's going to hurt for a good long while, but I know how to deal with that now. I'm just sorry I wasn't able to be there for you after. Toby's probably upset with me that I wasn't," she suggested.

"You know that's not true."

"Still, maybe if I'd been there with you, this wouldn't be happening to you."

I shrugged my shoulders. "I don't want to wish this away," I told her while patting my belly.

"No, you don't. And I hope you don't mind me being around more. I promise, I'll be the best surrogate auntie you and your baby could ask for. I know you have Ever, but I'd like to think we would have been sisters if…" I reached over and hugged her. I had been the only person in the family who knew about Gretchen and Toby being together. I'd seen them out at the movies one day and had been immediately sworn to secrecy about their relationship. Gretchen had been worried that Ever would hate her if she started dating Toby and the two of them wanted to give it a go to see if it would lead anywhere before telling everyone. I understood and promised to keep quiet, but I also got to hang out with the two of them periodically. I would never trade those memories, because it was during that time that I had finally grown closer to my big brother in a way I had always been envious of him having with Ever.

"You are a sister of my heart, Gretchen. No matter what." That did it, and the dam broke. Her tears fell, and began to soak through my shirt as we held onto one another and cried over my brother, her baby, and all that she'd lost, as well as the fact that I still counted her as family. "Hasn't Ever told you the same?"

"I'll be honest, I don't talk to her that much anymore. At first, I felt like I was betraying her when I started dating your brother. Then after everything, I couldn't look at her without breaking down. She started giving me space after about the fourth time, and told me when I was ready she would be there."

"You haven't been ready?"

"No, I have been for a while now, it's just that now I feel like a bit of brat for behaving the way I did towards her."

"She understands. I promise you, if anyone understands needing to get over hurts in your own way, and your own time, it's my sister." I was still sort of floored that I was sitting here speaking to Gretchen, the girl who my brother had been expecting a child with when he was killed and she ended up losing the baby. They had been heading home to tell our parents and my sister about everything during a family dinner that evening. Gretchen and Toby's romance had not been a secret from me though, and while me knowing about them added depth to my relationship with Toby, it also fostered a surrogate big sister in Gretchen for me. Ever had still been going through some things with our father and the club, and she didn't want to taint their opinion of me by being around me too often.

"What's going on?" Another female called out, though she was close enough that it startled me out of Gretchen's arms. I wasn't sure how I had missed someone walking up to us.

"Sweet baby Jesus, Beth, can you stop that ninja thing you do? You nearly scared Anna's baby right out of her," Gretchen chastised.

"Anna?" Her sister questioned. "Anna as in…"

I watched as Gretchen rolled her eyes at her sister. "Yes, Toby's little sister."

The woman, who didn't look much like Gretchen at all, tossed a hand up on her hip and glanced between the two of us then. "I thought she was a really little sister, as in under age to be carrying a baby?"

"Maybe I should just go," I said while standing to do just that. Even while standing, Beth's height was quiet intimidating. She had to be just shy of six feet tall, and while lacking the curves her pixie of a sister had, she was still built like an athlete.

"Oh, no you don't. Beth, you behave!" Gretchen chastised before she turned to speak to me again. "Please, don't go. Beth was just caught off guard with you being here, because up until this morning, I had just been saying I still wasn't ready to see you guys." I felt guilty at my sudden appearance in her life again knowing that she felt that way. I was about to apologize, but something in Gretchen's face stopped me. "I'm glad you came by because it proved how silly I have been. I missed you so much, and now seeing you here and talking to you, I think it would have helped me heal a bit more if I had just gotten myself together and come to see you."

"I'm sorry for snapping, and seeming judgmental for a minute there," Beth apologized to me, drawing my attention away from her sister. "I can see Gretchen means what she's saying. I thought maybe you were forcing yourself on her, and I wasn't ready for her to spiral back down into the dark place we just managed to get her to crawl out of." She stepped forward and held her hand out to me. "I'm Elizabeth, Gretchen's sister, but you can call me Beth."

I took her hand and shook it. "Anna, and don't worry, I think it's completely understandable to want to protect your sister," I informed her. "Honestly," I pointed to the window for the second time that day. "I didn't even know who owned this place. I just saw the sign, and figured I'd come check on the job. It's not like I haven't had enough rejections in the past four days of job hunting." I shrugged my shoulders up and down before smiling at her. "I thought, what could another one hurt before I headed home?"

"Oh, you poor thing. What kind of jobs have you been trying

for?" I told both her and Gretchen where I had applied and then pointed to my little baby bump. "Most of the rejections I received were while someone was staring at my little problem here." I realized how that might sound, and corrected myself quickly. "Not that the baby is a problem for me, but prospective employers seem to think it is."

"Have you ever had a job before?"

"No, but I learn fast, I'm friendly, and I'm super organized. I was also on the yearbook staff at school for two years."

"You're hired."

"I understand," I returned by rote. Then watched the puzzled faces looking back at me before Beth's actual words sunk in. "Wait, I'm hired? For real? Oh my God! Thank you! Thank you! Thank you!" Before she knew what was happening, I was basically tackle-hugging Beth. She just giggled along with her sister. "You look nothing like Gretchen by the way," I said as I had to crane my head way back to look up at her from that close.

Beth laughed again. "We have different fathers. Mine was a giant and hers was a dwarf," she teased. Gretchen was laughing along with her and it took her a minute to catch her breath.

"She always tells people that, but my dad is much larger than hers. If you looked up Viking on the internet, he would be the poster child. He was white-blonde hair, ice blue eyes, and stands at nearly six feet, five inches. She rolled her eyes. He's huge. I think if he hadn't required her to get a paternity test he never would have believed I was his spawn."

"That's crazy. I guess you take after your mom then?"

"Not really. She's not exactly short for a woman," Gretchen admitted.

"We just call her runt," Beth teased. "She takes after our grandma, who was a tiny thing until the day she died. The good part about that for Gretch is that she will probably never have to diet like the rest of the world."

"You don't look like you need to diet either," I suggested.

"Flattery will get you everywhere in this job. Can you start today?"

"Sure. My sister has appointments today until six, so I have until then."

"Is your car broken down?" Gretchen asked.

"I sold it to help with the baby expenses." I noticed the worried look on Beth's face. "Don't worry. My husband said I can use his truck if I need to."

"Husband?" Beth hissed out. "You're still a child. That sounds so wrong."

"It's in title only for insurance and so the baby will get his name, I guess." I honestly didn't know why he agreed to this anymore. Ever explained that our father could have kept me on his insurance. I was pretty sure you didn't need to be married to give a child their father's last name. Then again, I'd been wrong about a lot lately. Who knew?

"Where should we start?" I finally asked, breaking the silent staring thing the sisters had going on.

"Right," Beth puffed out before taking off toward the back. "Follow me. We'll get the paperwork out of the way first. Then we'll discuss pay, hours, and I'll show you how to run the appointment software. Tomorrow we can go over how to locate client files so you can show them their proofs while I'm working behind the camera." She grinned back at me then. "Just be glad we're living in the digital age. Back when my dad did this type of work, a pregnant woman would not have been welcome due to the chemicals used in the dark room. Since I don't use a darkroom – at least not here at the studio – you'll be fine. There's no heavy lifting on your part, and nothing strenuous to worry about. You should be able to work here through your whole pregnancy until you're no longer comfortable. When you need to take maternity leave, I'll just get a temp in here to fill in until you can come back. If you decide not to come back, all I ask is that you give me plenty of notice."

"That won't be a problem. I'll need a job after the baby is born too. Besides, I think I'll love working here. I have a really good feeling about this."

"So do I," Beth agreed before turning and moving toward the back again. I quickly followed behind her, eager to both learn something new and feel like I belonged somewhere again.

Chapter 9

The knock on my door pulled me out of the thoughts that

had been running rampant in my head. I came home from work during lunch again to find Anna gone. It had been a month since we were married and we barely saw each other. Granted, most of that was my fault since I was working doubles in order to bring in as much cash as I could between now and when the baby would be born. The problem was, when Deck asked me how Anna was doing a week ago, I couldn't give him an honest answer. It had been three days since I'd seen her. When she was home, she locked the bedroom door so I couldn't get in there with her. I had moved some of my clothes into a suitcase in the living room as a result, because she would often be asleep when I needed to get to my closet. There was no way I'd ever be able to repair the damage I'd done to us, or even hope to slap a bandage on it, if we never crossed paths.

When I opened the door, it was to find an excited Ever standing there bouncing on the balls of her feet. "Well?" She asked.

"Well, what?" I returned.

Her smile slipped into a scowl almost seamlessly. "Well, are you going to let me in?" I stepped out of the way so that she could come inside. I didn't miss the way her face wrinkled when she noticed my blankets were still on the couch and I had a suitcase in the middle of the floor. "It's been a month." The words came out so quietly, I had no doubt she hadn't meant to voice them out loud. She turned back to me with a questioning gaze, but I didn't possess the answers she was searching for so I simply shrugged it off and moved toward the kitchen. My stomach growled even though I didn't have an appetite. It was a reminder that I needed to eat though, even when I didn't feel up to it. I'd lost a few pounds in the past month, and I wasn't happy with the results. Normally, I would have hit the gym to bulk back up, but I'd need to add food to my diet before burning extra calories I didn't have to lose first.

"Where is Anna?" Ever finally asked as she glanced around the space, taking everything in.

"Your guess is as good as mine. I've been coming home at lunch time every day this week trying to catch her, but she's never here."

"What do you mean she's never here? And what do you mean by trying to catch her?"

"I haven't actually laid eyes on your sister in about six days, and before that, it was only because she happened to come out of the bedroom before I left for work since I was running late that day."

"I don't understand. She said everything was going fine."

"I guess if her idea of fine is never seeing me, then she wasn't exactly lying," I informed Ever.

"Why the hell didn't you go to the doctor's appointment with her?" Ever's accusatory tone was starting to piss me off.

"What fucking doctor's appointment?" I threw the anger-laced words back at her and she blanched. Once again, I had no clue what she was talking about.

"That's why I'm here. I couldn't go earlier because I had an appointment with an asshole who refused to reschedule, but I couldn't turn the work down either. It's probably going to be an award winning piece." I just glared in her general direction, because I could give a fuck less about her work when I was trying to figure out why I hadn't been invited to a doctor's appointment for my own baby.

"Ever, get back on track. What doctor's appointment?"

"She really didn't tell you about it? She was going to be able to find out the sex of the baby today and everything," she chirped happily until she remembered I knew nothing about that.

"No, she didn't tell me about it." I felt my temper rising as each word was spit out past my clenched teeth.

"What is going on that you live with my sister, but don't seem to know anything going on with her?"

I laughed at Ever then. There was no humor in the sound, and yet there wasn't a more appropriate response, because this had to be fucking joke. "Are you seriously asking me that? Don't you think that's a better question for your sister instead of me?"

"She's not here to ask," Ever pointed out.

"I don't know what her deal is. I just told you, every time I try to be here to catch her while she's here, and not locked up in that room, the truck is missing from the driveway. I've been working a lot of overtime trying to save up because babies are expensive and insurance doesn't cover anything. Though, I don't know exactly what I need to cover either, because I didn't even know she had a doctor appointment." My nostrils flared with the words that grew louder and angrier as I spat each one out.

"This isn't okay," Ever stated quietly.

"No shit!" I hissed at her. "None of this is fucking okay. I tried to talk to her when she first moved in. I thought we were going to be okay. Granted, I figured it would take a while to get to a good place, but still… It's been a goddamn month and I'm still waiting to talk to her again. That's my baby she's carrying. I should at least know about appointments even if she doesn't want me there. From what you're saying, she probably knows about the sex of the baby and she's out there with that knowledge while I'm here not even knowing that it was a possibility."

"I'm sorry, Joker. You're right. That isn't okay. Let me see if I can get a hold of her." Before Ever could get the number dialed on her cell phone, the front door opened and a beaming Anna walked in the living room of my house. She wasn't alone as I expected though. A blonde little pixie walked in right behind her. Both of them were laughing before they looked up, obviously startled to see us here. It was then I realized Ever must have parked on the street instead of the driveway. She must have been afraid to block me in. Granted, I would have thought the two women who seemed stunned to see people in the house should have noticed my bike parked in the carport.

"Gretchen?" Ever asked, obviously the first to be pulled from the surprised stupor everyone else had fallen into.

"Hey, Ever," the pixie responded shyly, ignoring me completely.

"What are you doing with Anna?"

"Am I not supposed to talk to her?" Gretchen countered defensively.

"I just didn't realize you were friendly." I didn't miss the wounded tone in Ever's words.

"Well, she works at my sister's studio so we've become friends."

"You work?" Ever asked her sister. "When did you get a job? Why? Is there something you needed?" Ever directed the question to her sister, but then turned accusatory eyes back on me. Great. I was the bad guy again. Never mind the fact that she didn't even know her own sister had a job. Hell, I didn't even know my own wife had a fucking job, a doctor's appointment, or anything else at this point. Tomorrow I'd probably wake to find I'd already been divorced and missed it happening somehow.

Gretchen glanced around the room warily, guilt obvious in her features, as she realized she had just let the cat out of the bag. Anna didn't look bothered one bit though.

"I got the job a couple weeks ago after I moved in."

"Why?" I asked, speaking for the first time since the women had walked through my door.

She sighed and then sat down and took her shoes off while frowning. Anna started to rub her obviously sore feet. "I needed to be able to save some money. Baby stuff is expensive," she told us, mirroring my excuse for working more hours. "Besides, apartment aren't cheap and I needed to be able to get a head start on saving for one so that if anything happens and I'm out of work too long, I can still afford to pay my bills."

"Apartment? What the hell? You're moving out?" I felt like I'd just started watching a movie at the mid-way point. I was so confused about what was happening in my own life, and now I had frustrated, hurt, and angry to add to the mix with all the revelations coming my way.

"I told you I didn't want to be a burden. You're displaced on the couch and you can't be comfortable bringing women home with a pregnant wife living here," she added at the end, sending a spear of pain to lance through my heart. My hand immediately lifted to try to massage away the ache in my chest and it took everything for me not to double over the hit she had just given me.

"What?" Ever yelled at the same time Gretchen turned her steely eyes on me and demanded, "What the fuck?"

I ignored them both and stared at Anna. "You're my wife," I told her slowly so she could comprehend. "You're my responsibility along with the baby you're carrying. I have the bills covered and no woman, beyond you, Ever, and now Gretchen has ever even been to my house before. I wouldn't bring one here anyway. I wouldn't even be with anyone else because you. Are. My. Wife!"

She swished her hand in the air as if to bat my words away. "Everyone know our marriage wasn't real," she stated.

"It's so real that it's legally binding, sweetheart," I spat at her, unable to control myself any longer.

She looked like she was about to say something. I saw the lively spark in her eye, a flash of something – fury maybe – that I'd never seen before. Instead she shook it off. "We don't even share a bedroom, let alone have sex, and you're not exactly faithful, so let's not play pretend here – that's what made you mad at me in the first place, right?"

This was not the same Anna sitting before me. She wasn't pulling any punches. What was I supposed to say to any of that? It was all true, even if it didn't feel right. "Anna, this freeze out has to stop," I demanded. "What if something happened to you? No one would know. What if something happened to the baby? You didn't even tell me about the appointment you had. That's my baby in there. I should at least know that you saw a doctor, or get an update if you don't want me there. Instead, I have to worry and use my imagination because you don't tell me shit!"

"When am I supposed to tell you? You're gone all the time."

"No, I'm not. You just decided to hide from me when I am around."

"Well," she started to argue but her sister cut her off.

"Put the shoe on the other foot, little sister. If he was carrying the baby wouldn't you want to know? This is part of growing up and realizing that the things concerning your child aren't just about you. Don't do to your baby what my parents did to me."

"What do you mean?" Anna asked Ever.

"My biological mother turned my father into a ghost in my life, never talking about him, and look what happened when I lost her. I was sent to live with strangers. Then I was hated by my own father and his club brothers because of who my mom was. I had no control over who my parents were or what they did or didn't feel for one another, but they all could have done me a favor and not punished me for their own bullshit decisions. Make no mistake – if you use that baby as a means to hurt him, you're ultimately hurting your child too. They'll feel that."

I watched as Anna's lip began to quiver and her hand moved protectively over her stomach. She only met my eyes for a brief moment before mumbling the word sorry and running from the room.

"Shit!" Ever started to go after her, but Gretchen grabbed hold of her arm to keep her back.

"She'll be fine. She's just hormonal right now," the woman assured her. Then she turned to me. "I understand your situation isn't ideal but you could try harder too. Pull her out of hiding and make her talk to you."

"I won't ever make her do anything," I told her through gritted teeth.

"Well, then you'll probably lose them both."

"Why can't she just grow the fuck up? I admitted to being an asshole. I apologized. And still she can't even tell me about an appointment to see the baby?"

"Maybe you should also grow the fuck up and try asking her about it."

"She's already got a foot out the door, a thousand reasons plucked from whatever fantasy is in her head, and it's all on my shoulders to get her to talk?"

Gretchen shrugged. "You both need to grow up and realize you have more to worry about than just yourselves."

"Get out!" I finally yelled, losing it. Part of the fucking problem with Anna and me seemed to be with everyone else inserting themselves in our lives and giving advice when they didn't even understand what the hell was actually going on. Hell, other people's opinions are why she felt she had to lie to me to begin with.

"Get the fuck out if you think that's what's going on. I'm half-assed sleeping on a couch to appease her. I have a bed at the clubhouse but I can't use it because God forbid she think I'm fucking someone in it. Why should I care though? Apparently, she thinks that anyway. I'm working doubles to make sure we can afford baby shit, so being gone all those hours gets translated to I'm sleeping around too.

"Then she gets a job and tells no one about it. She goes to

the doctor and leaves me in the dark, she fucking hides from me and ignores when I try to ask about the baby or her when she accidentally runs into me if I'm late leaving for work. She literally has my schedule timed so she's locked away or not here when I am. I can't sleep at night for trying to figure out how to turn this around, but you're gonna march your happy ass in my house and presume I'm being selfish? Based on what? Bullshit she's telling you without telling you that she's causing her own misery at this point?" Both Gretchen and Ever stood looking shell-shocked at my tirade. I didn't want to see their faces any longer though. I was tired. Physically warn out from working doubles and sleeping on a couch not meant to be a permanent bed, and then the mental exhaustion were both bringing me to my knees.

"You know what? I'm fucking done here. I'm exhausted and I can't fix shit alone. I can't change the past or her mind, but I won't continue being punished for caring or for trying." I turned to Ever then. "You should probably go ahead and make room for her at your place. I'll help get her set up with a place of her own once the baby is here. Hell, fuck it, she can have the house. I'll move my shit out. I won't be the reason she stays miserable and everyone blames me."

"Maybe you should give this some thought," Ever stated calmly.

"I did. It's all I've done."

"Okay." She moved across the room and pulled out her

phone. I knew she was calling Deck. I didn't bother listening in on that conversation, because honestly, I didn't have it in me to care any longer. What was the point? I'd fucked up enough that there was no fixing the situation and Anna had just finally proven that to me.

"I'll send her out here while I pack my shit up," I told Ever as I moved to go to the bedroom that once had been mine. The same bedroom I'd once dreamed of sharing with a beautiful girl I'd called Lise at the time.

I opened the door, which was surprisingly unlocked. "The girls are waiting for you out there," I mentioned before moving to the closet where most of my things were still kept. I pulled a duffle bag down from the top shelf and started rolling my clothes and stuffing them inside.

"This is your house," Anna insisted as she sat there on the edge of the bed watching me instead of going out to the living room where her sister and friend were waiting.

"Nah, it's ours. I put it in both our names after we married." That was a surprise to her judging by the shocked look she was giving me. "I'll have my name taken off. I bought this house free and clear of debt when I came out of the military. You won't have to worry about rent or a mortgage," I informed her. "Though I will stipulate that you can't sell it. The house can pass to our child when they're old enough, but I want to ensure they always have a place to call home."

"The baby is fine," she whispered so low I almost missed it. "I heard the heartbeat today, nothing else. The machine they were supposed to use was broken. They rescheduled the rest of the appointment," she mentioned with a little more excitement in her voice.

I'd missed it. I felt so far removed from the pregnancy, it was honestly nothing more than a remote idea for me. I turned my back on her when I felt the telling burn in my eyes. Fuck! Fuck! Fuck! I continued stuffing things in my duffle while trying to calm my emotions.

"I didn't think you'd care." Her words continued to gut me.

"If I didn't care, you never would have been here."

"I'm only here because my daddy threatened you and most likely your standing in the club."

I turned, anger taking over. "You think so? Maybe you need to go talk to your daddy then. He suggested it in anger, but retracted his requirement of marriage the next day. He said he'd never do to you what Tiger Lily's dad put her and Merc through."

"But,"

"I told him I wanted it so our kid wouldn't have to be handed off like a pawn in a game on visitation days. I was still mad at you, but I knew I'd regret not trying."

"I didn't know that," she said meekly.

"Well, now you do," I told her as I stuffed the last of the

clothes I wore regularly into the bag, sealed it up, and left her there in the house with Ever and Gretchen.

I found myself on Merc's doorstep a little while later begging for a place to stay where I knew rumors and wild imaginations wouldn't come back to bite me in the ass.

Chapter 10

DEARY
DIARY

I stared down at the words I'd left marring the page of my

journal. It has been a long time since I'd felt like writing, but today I had to get it all off my chest.

Dear Diary,

I thought the house was cold and unkind before he left, but with each day that passes where I'm the only occupant – other than my baby I'm growing – my heart squeezes with the loneliness I feel, like a cloak it's doomed to stay wrapped in.

I had taken for granted just how big his presence was here. It has been six days since he walked out promising the house was mine to keep. I hadn't heard a single word from him. When he told the girls he was done, I didn't think he meant it. Now, I was positive he had. My days since consisted of going to work, coming home, and then crying myself to sleep and crashing every night. Every once in a while, I'd glance down at my empty ring finger and wish for a different life. The life I used to dream I'd have before I made one lousy decision that cost me everything. All because I was too impatient to wait like Toby asked me to do.

My wonderful older brother had been the only person paying attention when he saw me watching Evan at a club family cookout. That's where he was introduced to the club and Deck informed Merc that he was going to sponsor the man who wanted to prospect for the club. "Don't even think about it, little sister," my brother had told me. "He's too old for you, and he wants to join the club. If you try going after him now, you'll ruin his chances of becoming a member."

"I can't ruin anything if he doesn't want me the same way, T-Bone," I told him purposely calling him by his road name because I wanted him, to know that I understood he was speaking to me as a club ambassador as much as from the perspective of older brother.

"Anna, it's not like that. I just don't want to see you get hurt. You, my darling little sis, have only seen everyone's good behavior in the clubhouse, because you're not allowed to be here after hours. Trust me when I say, our dad is a shining example for how to treat your woman. Many of these other men are not."

"They hurt women?" I had asked him, not able to fathom that the gentlemen I'd grown up knowing as my uncles would ever be able to lay a hand on a woman in anger.

"Not physically, sis. Maybe not even intentionally. How would you feel if you dated that guy only to walk into the clubhouse one day and see him with one of the club whores?"

"I would hope that no man I would date would do that," I told him honestly.

"Yeah me too. Now imagine if that happened and someone saw him doing it, or you told someone. You think any of the older men, J-Bird, Deck, or me would allow that to happen unchecked?"

"I guess not."

"No, we wouldn't. So then you'd have a broken heart and we'd have a rift in the club where one of the brothers was concerned."

"He's not even a member," I argued.

"Not yet, but Deck sponsored him in tonight. He starts prospecting tomorrow. Besides, You barely just turned 17. You're not old enough. Someone catching wind of him dating

you before you turned 18 would mean an automatic no from the club."

I remember poking my lip out then. It hadn't been the first time I'd seen Deck bring the man around. Not that he had ever noticed me though. I always managed to get sent home before anything fun happened at the clubhouse, and Deck and Ever didn't bother showing up there until late in the evenings when they did go hang out because Ever worked so late at the tattoo studio. Evan couldn't be there without Deck. At least he couldn't until he started prospecting, which apparently was going to be tomorrow since they'd voted to bring him on today. That was what this party was all about. Two new prospects were brought in today.

"It's time for you to go home, sis."

"I know," I whined to Toby as I turned to head to the door and out to my car. My brother walked me to my car and saw me inside.

"I'm going to need that promise from you," he told me. When I just stared at him blankly, he tried again. "If you're still interested and you're both single when you turn 18, I will have your back and make sure the brothers stay out of your way if it's something you both want."

"Really?" I'd asked apprehensively. "You would do that for me?"

"I'm not making any promises for him, Anna. That's only

if he meets you and wants that too. Keep your head out of the clouds about him. Fantasy and reality rarely meet up in the way we think they will."

"Whatever." I'd dismissed him with a little attitude and a quick punch to his shoulder. "Thanks, Toby."

"Love you, squirt!"

"Love you too," I told him, and then I'd driven from the clubhouse to our home where I broke part of my promise. I started daydreaming about the day when Evan and I would be together. I dreamed of our marriage, and the children we would have. A boy that looked like him and girl that resembled me.

My marriage – the real thing – was nothing like what I'd imagined all those many months ago. It had almost been a year now since I had that conversation with my big brother. He would be so disappointed in me. My marriage was only a piece of paper signed by two people. There were no rings exchanged. No kisses to seal the deal. We only had the one picture of Joker's hand and part of my silhouette. He had put his hand up to keep anyone from taking wedding pictures for us. Ever had snuck that one in on my phone, but honestly you couldn't even see either of our faces in it. Then there was the other picture taken on our wedding night. The one that showed in vivid detail that one of us also did not get to indulge in the consummation part of the wedding night. Considering that was the case, I could probably have the marriage annulled like it never happened. It was something to think about.

I never would have guessed I would be turning 18 all alone with a baby in my belly and a divorce on the way. So much for all my dreams I wrote about in this stupid diary. My brother was right. Reality didn't meet my expectations. It killed them, along with the dreams I'd had for my future.

I must have fallen asleep rereading the words in my diary, because when I woke, my cheek rested on the open page and there was a telling wetness to the paper. I'd like to say it was from tears that had leaked from my eyes at the loss of my dreams, but I was pretty sure my tear ducts were all dried out at this point. Instead, I had to be embarrassed because it was definitely drool marking my paper, and the reason I had been startled awake was standing in front of me smiling at the sight I made. Ugh.

"Hi," he said as he attempted to hide his smile.

"Hi," I parroted while trying to shake off the grogginess. I moved to sit up and tucked my diary away in the backpack sitting at me feet.

"Were you working on homework?"

"No, something else. Is there something you need?"

"Yes," he finally said before taking a seat across from me in the chair.

"Okay, what is it? Do you need me to move out now?"

"No. I told you the house is yours, Anna."

"What do we need to talk about then?"

"I wanted to make sure you had everything you need. I was paying the utility bills today, and it reminded me that there were other things you might need. I don't know when your make-up appointment is, but if you let me know how much…"

"You paid the utility bills?" I asked.

He grinned at me. "Yes, that's why the lights stay on."

I felt a little sick. I was already failing at this adulting thing. "I didn't even think about it," I admitted.

"Why would you? You've never had to pay them before." He shrugged it off like it was nothing. In reality, it was everything. He was still taking care of me even when I had refused to tell him about appointments and had been a brat. He had been right that day when he yelled at my sister and Gretchen. I had been purposely avoiding him every step of the way. I never allowed him to speak to me long enough to even ask more than a simple, 'how are you?'.

When I didn't say anything else, the slip of a smile on his face vanished and he stood again. "Okay, well, I'll get out of your way then. I just wanted to check in and let you know that's been taken care of so you wouldn't be worried. If you need anything, shoot me a text."

I laughed at that. It sounded like the most empty promise I'd been handed outside of our wedding vows.

"What's so funny?"

"You wanting me to text you."

"What exactly is funny about that? I meant it."

I continued to laugh, but with each heaving breath I took as a result the laughter turned to me choking on sobs instead. These hormones were dooming me to eternal humiliation.

"Anna? What the hell?"

It took a minute, but I was able to pull myself together enough to let him know why me texting him about my troubles was about as ridiculous and pointless as me writing in my stupid drool-stained journal. "I'd have to know your number in order to text you, Joker."

A look akin to horror and surprise crossed his face at the mention of the fact that I didn't have a number I could text to get a hold of him other than through a third party, I supposed. If I was going to go through someone else, I'd just tell them my troubles instead.

"Shit! I thought I had given it to you." He seemed to be trying to remember the moment when he supposedly gave it to me, but I knew better. That moment never happened. "I remember talking about it with Deck," he told me as he glanced back down at me looking puzzled still. "I'm sorry, Anna. I didn't realize." He asked me to get my phone out then, and rattled off his new number. I put it in my cell. "Now text me really quick so I know you got the right one in there."

"I'm not stupid," I scolded.

"Not saying you are, beautiful. I hit the wrong numbers often. It happens."

I didn't respond to him calling me beautiful. Instead, I texted him.

Me: This is not the wrong number.

His phone dinged with the incoming text and when he read it, he laughed, making me feel warm inside to see that response from him for the first time in far too long. I used to love making him laugh because it made his eyes shine so brightly when he did. Joker was a man who was born to smile, laugh, and make people happy. I felt like I had destroyed a part of that when I wasn't honest with him about who I was, and I'd been swimming in that guilt ever since.

"I see you got the text this time, Joker," I insisted.

"I don't like when you do that," he told me.

"Do what?"

"Call me Joker. It doesn't seem right coming from you."

"Why not?"

"Because you used to call me Evan."

"You used to call me something different too," I admitted, bringing up my shameful mistake.

"That was out of necessity for you, not what you really wanted me to call you, right?" I tipped my head up and down in agreement before he continued on. "Well, I liked you calling me Evan. I wish you would again." I felt the blush burn hot on my cheeks. One of the last times I'd spoken his name had been when we were having sex and I'd called out his name. He smiled warmly at me, his eyes going molten the way they did when he was aroused before. Clearly, he had been remembering the same thing. "I'd like for us to not be strangers to one another anymore, Anna. I want to be friends at the very least, but if I'm being honest. It kills me not to be involved with stuff going on with the baby. I don't know what it will take to get you to come around about that, but you have to let me in. I don't even feel like it's real. It's just something everyone keeps talking about to me. I don't want to be a stranger in my child's life."

"I know, and I'm sorry. I honestly wasn't doing it to hurt you so much as protect me."

"I would never hurt you," he started to say. "Not intentionally, and definitely never physically."

"I'll do better, I promise." I reached into the bookbag that was still sitting at my feet and grabbed my appointment card out of it. "Here," I told him as his fingers brushed over my own before he took hold of the card.

"What is this?"

"My next appointment, so you know when and where to be there."

He took his phone out and took a picture of it before trying to hand it back. "Keep it. I already have it in my calendar. He nodded and then just stared at the card for a really long time. It was in that moment I realized how much I had truly messed up about the appointments. I could see how much it meant to him, and the guilt swam through me again at the thought that I'd denied him the ability to get to know his child in the same ways I was.

"I cry every time I hear the baby's heartbeat," I admitted. "You would think maybe just the first time, but every time I hear that quick little flutter of sound, it's like magic." His eyes shifted from the card to meet mine as he listened to what I was saying. "I don't want to know what the sex is even though they're supposed to be able to tell me at this appointment."

"Why not?"

"There aren't too many real surprises left in the world. I want this to be one of them," I explained as I patted my belly.

"I think I'd rather know so I can get prepared. I'd hate for people to buy a bunch of pink stuff and it end up being a boy."

"I'm pretty sure people stick to neutral colors for babies when they don't know the gender," I assured him. He didn't seem convinced.

"Are you scared?" He asked me out of the blue after we'd sat in silence for a few minutes.

"Every single day. I'm afraid of giving birth. I'm worried something will happen to the baby before I can, or while I try. I'm scared to death that I'll die trying and never get to hold my own child or see them grow up. I'm terrified that I will be a

141

horrible mom. Pretty much everything about having a baby frightens me to death."

He moved from his chair then and sat down right next to me, pulling me to his body and wrapping his arms around. We sat there just rocking back and forth in each other's arms for a few minutes before he spoke. "I'm worried about all those things too, and then I get to top it off with the fact that I've pissed you off enough that I'll never be able to be a part of your lives. That's the worst feeling."

"I'm sorry for making you feel that way. That's not what I want, I promise. This whole thing has been so confusing. It's like I got on a runaway train and I've been trying to get off at my stop, but every time I do, the train speeds up and passes by my instead. You know?"

"I know that feeling too, Anna. I'm sick of that feeling. What do you say we take over the controls and throw the break for a while? Let's start out building things up between us again and see where we end up. What do you say? It has to be better than the never ending nightmare ride we're both on."

"That's true," I agreed.

"Good," he sighed out and I could tell by the way his body relaxed that he meant it. He wanted a fresh start to try to see what kind of a relationship, if any, we could manage to have and I'd be a liar if I said I didn't want that too. I wasn't sure if we would end up like Tiger Lily and Merc, happily ever after, but I hoped we could at least learn to be friends for our child's sake.

"Have you thought of any names yet?" He asked me and I turned to him, wondering if he had.

"Not really. I didn't want to jinx anything. I thought about just naming the baby when it's born. You know, seeing the little person in my arms before I decide."

"You're putting a lot of weight on our shoulders at the end aren't you? Waiting to find out the sex, waiting to name the baby now too? Come on, there has to be a name or two rolling around in your head already. Every girl dreams of what they'll name their children one day, don't they?"

I shook my head. "No. I never dreamed about their names because I thought that was something their father and I would figure out together one day."

"Their?" He asked causing me to blush profusely. "You want more than one?"

"Well, if we're talking my dreams, I thought I'd be married first, so that's out the window."

"Technically, you're married before the baby will be born."

"Yes, but I'm talking about being married to a man who loves me and wants a family with me. So, the additional kids I wanted wouldn't be an issue. Now, I don't know. I feel like I'll be another one of those women who is always judged horribly for having more than one dad for my kids. Not to mention the dynamics. I don't want one child preferred over the others in my home simply because of genetics." I stopped my rambling when it looked like Joker might get sick. "Are you okay?"

"Yeah, that's a lot to take in. Anna, I know our start has been less than perfect, and we're just getting to the point where we can talk about things…"

"But?"

"But every time I hear you talk about the future, it's like a forgone conclusion that your future won't have me in it. First, the apartment you were saving for. Now, you're already talking about another father for your future children. Did I screw things up so horribly already that there's not even a hint of a chance that it will be me in that family picture you're drawing in your mind?"

How was I supposed to respond to that? "I, um, I guess I didn't think you would want to be in the picture. Other than being this baby's father, obviously," I tacked on so as not to leave him out of that. "You haven't acted like you want me around, or that you even like me, so I've assumed you were just counting down until we didn't have to be married anymore."

"That's not true," he insisted.

My brows raised in surprise and he huffed out a frustrated breath before running his hands through the hair that had started growing longer since we were together. It was curling at the ends now where it was starting to hand down his neck a little. I liked him with the fresh military cut, but he had a different sort of appeal like this too.

"I know that I didn't behave well at the wedding we had, and I can't apologize enough for that. I was still angry with you then, and hadn't taken the time to see things from your perspective. I realized after speaking to Deck and Merc that you had pretty good reasons for doing what you did, and that if the shoe were on the other foot I might have done the same. Well, probably not the same, but you know what I'm getting at. I understand now. I don't hate you, Anna. I don't hold anything against you either. The only person between the two of us I'm angry with still is myself for fucking things up so much worse than they needed to be because I couldn't swallow my damn pride sooner."

"Okay," I told him. "Well, we agreed to see where things go. I think it's best if we leave the dreams of the future on hold outside of hoping for a healthy, happy little baby." I offered him a small smile. "Let's just see where things go from there. I'd really like to be friends with you again."

"We were never friends, Anna."

"We have to be now though, for the baby."

"What if I want there to be more? I miss the way we were together in the beginning. You captivated me, Anna."

"I don't think that's a good idea right now. I thought we were going to make this a process and work on starting from down at the bottom of the barrel before crawling out and starting over in a completely new one?"

He grinned. "Where's your sense of adventure."

I pointed to my belly. "This happened the last time I got adventurous. Now, I'll take the safe path to make sure I'm doing right by my baby. It's one less thing for me to fear when I close my eyes at night."

Joker pulled me into another hug then. "Okay, Anna. We'll do this your way. I don't want to continue being strangers though. Never seeing you, or knowing what's going on with you, it's been killing me."

"Why don't you just move back in so we can work on getting to know one another again. It seems like the only way that's going to happen since we both have pretty busy schedules right now." I couldn't believe that I had just spoken those words, and judging by the shocked expression on his face, neither could Joker.

"Are you serious?"

"Well, yes. I wouldn't have said it if I didn't mean it." When his eyes lit up with interest, I tacked on my caveat. "You still need to sleep in another room. I think you should take your room back and I'll just stay in the guest room. We don't need to take the bed out of there just yet."

"How about you stay right where you are since you're already comfortable and I'll take the guest room until the baby comes or we decide differently."

THE PRINCESS *and the* PROSPECT

I gave him a narrow-eyed appraisal at the suggestion that our living arrangements might change before the baby comes. It was clear that he meant for us to be sharing a bed. Though I couldn't for the life of me think of why he'd want that. I saw myself in the mirror every day. Pregnancy was not doing nice things to my body. Well, It had filled out my boobs quite nicely, but other than that, I was just starting to look like I was smuggling a small melon under my shirt, topped off by two oversized apples, maybe large oranges. Crap. I was hungry. "I need to eat." I stood and moved to the kitchen.

"That was weird," he told me as he followed me to the kitchen.

"Um, I just thought of melons and apples and it hit me."

"Why were you thinking of fruit in the middle of our conversation about me moving in?"

I shrugged my shoulders playing it off. "I don't know. I'm pregnant. My weird hormone stuff is always messing with my train of thought."

"That's a real thing?"

"Sure it is," I told him as I turned my back to make sure he couldn't see the grin on my face.

"I can see your reflection in the window," he pointed out as his cell phone dinged. Well, shoot. I guess I was busted. It wasn't exactly a lie. Pregnancy was making me feel and act weird. Just yesterday I ate a peanut butter and grilled cheese sandwich and washed it down with a strange apple juice and milk concoction. I'm surprised I didn't throw up. Old me would have tossed her cookies at just the thought. Pregnant me wolfed it down and wished for more. I didn't want to tell him that thought. I was embarrassed for myself.

I glanced over my shoulder when he grew quiet and didn't say anything more. He was staring at the text he'd received on his phone and whatever he was reading had his brows furrowed, and he looked sort of angry. "Everything okay?" I asked.

"Yeah, sorry," he told me as he tucked his phone back into his pocket. "That was Deck. I have to run to the clubhouse real quick. I'll be back in about an hour or so though, okay?"

"Sure," I told him and he was off and running out the door.

An hour and a half after he stormed out of the house, I heard the tell-tale sound of a car pulling up. I wasn't sure who it was because I didn't recognize the vehicle. Then I watched as Joker peeled himself out of the green Buick Skylark that looked as though it had seen better day, and moved the seat forward so he could pull something from the back seat. I turned away then, wondering what the hell he was up to. I knew for a fact that wasn't his car. He only had the motorcycle and the truck that I left parked under the carport. The way he bent into the backseat gave me flashbacks of him doing just that in my dreams to pluck our baby out of its car seat. A hot flash of anger and sadness whipped through my body at the thought that maybe he was bringing someone else's child here.

What if he already had a kid I didn't know about? Oh God! Panic took hold as I let my imagination spin out freely from one crazy scenario to another. Please, don't let him have another kid. That would mean he hadn't really been taking care of it, or at the very least that he was lying to me about a whole other part of his life this whole time. 'Please be baby brain anxiety. Please, be baby brain anxiety.' I chanted those words to myself on repeat until I heard him struggling with something on the front stoop.

The front door opened, but I was too afraid of what I'd find there to turn and look. Instead, I made myself busy in the kitchen cleaning the dirty dishes from my earlier mess. "Anna?" Joker called out forcing my attention to turn to him. When I did, the sight that greeted wasn't at all what I expected.

"What is all this?" I asked. He was standing in the doorway holding a hoard of balloons and what looked suspiciously like a personal sized ice cream cake. He answered only with a grin as he moved further into the house and kicked back with a foot to shut the door. He was by my side and leaned down to kiss my cheek.

"Happy birthday," he whispered into my ear before handing me the balloons and setting the cake down on the kitchen counter. My eyes immediately welled up. I thought everyone had forgotten, and here one of the people I didn't think knew my birthday was doing all of this.

"How did you know?"

"A little birdie told me," he responded.

"But everyone forgot this year," I managed to get out past the emotion that was clogging my throat.

He turned back to me just in time to see the first tear fall. Something passed over his face when he saw that, but I was too emotional to be able to decipher his expressions. "They didn't forget, beautiful. I asked them to come over tomorrow for a cookout and to celebrate. We really do have some club business going on right now that we need to see to. I can't even stay that long, but I wanted to make sure you didn't think you were forgotten."

"That was sweet of you."

His grin turned devilish then. "On a scale of one to ten, exactly how sweet was it?"

"It's going back down to a zero quickly," I informed him as I turned to look at the cake. It was just a small one, but it was one of my favorites. Ice cream cake with that yummy cookie crumble stuff in the middle. They never did use enough of the cookie crumble stuff for my liking, but whatever. Pregnant beggars couldn't be choosers and all that.

"I hope that's okay. I remember you telling me your brother had gone to your school and sneaked you a small one during lunch one year."

"He did." My words came out on a whisper as I was engulfed by memories of Toby doing just that. He had made my day and all of my friends had been incredibly envious. I ended up making new friends after that too. At least, I thought I had. It turned out they all just wanted me to hook them up with my brother or with one of the other guys from the club. As if any of the Aces High guys would touch their underage tails. I was so lost in the memories that I didn't even realize Joker had gotten closer to me. His arms wrapped around my body and then he pulled me into a warm hug while pressing a kiss to the top of my head.

"I didn't mean to bring up memories that would hurt you," he apologized.

"You didn't. I love the memory of him doing that for me. I just miss Toby so much. Hanging around with Gretchen once in a while has sort of eased that ache in a weird way, but it's not the same as having my big brother surprise me on my birthday. He used to do it every year while he let everyone else pretend they forgot." It was then that I glanced up into his eyes and realized what he had truly done. "Who told you?"

"Deck," he admitted. "I'm glad he did. I'm obviously not trying to move into big brother territory here, especially since you're already carrying my child, but I figured someone should step into Toby's shoes for the day and make your birthday just as special as he would have done."

I threw my arms around his waist and held on to the man so tightly it had to be uncomfortable for him. He never complained though. "Thank you, and thank Deck for me too."

"You can thank Deck tomorrow, beautiful." He leaned in and gave me one more kiss on the top of my head while sliding his hands from where they had rested on my back down lower on my hips and around to my belly. He glanced down between us at my growing belly as he cradled it while his fingers slid back and forth in what appeared to be reverence. How many times had I dreamed of the man doing just that? Too many to count and now it was happening. The moment nearly brought me to my knees, and just as quickly as it happened he was pulling away and backing up a step causing my own hands to fall from his hips to my sides. I glanced up to see moisture evident in his eyes before he turned his back to me and grabbed the cake from the counter.

"You best grab a slice of this and put the rest in the freezer before it melts any further. That car was an oven when I got in it."

"Whose car is that anyway? I've never seen it before."

"Just someone at the clubhouse. I realized a little too late that I wouldn't be able to travel too fast with a cake and balloons while on my bike."

"I would have loved to see that sight while driving down the road though," I teased.

"You and pretty much every asshole at the club. None of them would let me take their car. Not that many had cars at the clubhouse though." He pointed over his shoulder to the car outside. "Some hanger on with one of the brothers leant it to me so I need to go get it back and then tend to club business. Don't forget, we're partying tomorrow."

"Do I need to go get anything? I haven't exactly shopped for foods for a cookout."

"No, but if you don't have anything to do between now and then, I'd like to come back and grab my truck for a bit. I'll bring the stuff tomorrow, and it'll give me a way to get my things back here too, if you're still serious about that?"

"Of course I'm serious about that."

"Good then I'll see you later."

He didn't see me later.

I awoke wondering what today would actually bring. Joker had never returned last night. He had mentioned club business that needed to be handled, but I thought he'd be bringing his things back and staying at the house last night. I had apparently thought wrong though. He never came back, and never bothered to call or text either. All that hopefulness I'd felt the night before drained out of me again in the light of day that was streaming through my window. I honestly hoped he hadn't actually invited my family to come here today, and that he had only been running his mouth or trying to hurt me somehow. I didn't think I could face them. I felt like complete crap, and hadn't slept very well.

"You're not doing this to yourself again!" I scolded myself out loud and then stood, going to my closet to get some clothes for the day. As soon as I was done my shower I would call Gretchen and see if she wanted to hang out with me for the day.

Before I jumped in the shower, I went to the kitchen to grab a drink, and I saw a bunch of bags sitting on the counter along with a note.

> *Beautiful,*
>
> *I had to drop these off and run. Cold stuff is already in the fridge. I'll be back in a bit to help get things ready. Everyone should be showing up around noon. If you could make the potato salad, that would be great. If not, I got a bunch of chips – fuck everyone who wanted potato salad anyway!*
>
> *Yours,*
>
> *Evan*

My hand was shaking as I placed the note back down on the

table. My finger traced over the word "Beautiful" and then over the word "Yours". I wondered if he knew what he did to my battered heart with simple words like that? Probably not. I moved quickly from that point, because it was already getting close to 10 o'clock and that didn't leave me a lot of time to worry about throwing together potato salad, especially since I still had to cook the damn potatoes.

It was going on 11 in the morning when I finally had showered, gotten dressed, and had just finished up the potato salad as well as setting out the paper plates, napkins, and other things that Joker had purchased and left in bags on the counters. I had chips ready to pour into bowls, and even took a minute to eat some toast and drink a little juice in order to help settle my nervous stomach a bit. The last didn't really help. I kept feeling little flutters, almost like bubbles in my tummy. It was weird to experience because I wasn't usually a nervous person, recent panicky episodes aside.

I had just finished cleaning up my mess and tucking all the non-essential things away when there was a knock on the door. It was only quarter after 11, but I figured maybe Ever or my momma had come by a little early to help out. I still hadn't heard from Joker – other than the note on the counter – which was weird since he had put all of this together. I hoped everyone who showed up really liked potato salad and chips, because it was just about all I'd managed to put together. Those worries slipped away when I opened the door to see who was standing there. More importantly, I saw the same green Skylark parked on the road that had been there the day before too, when Joker had driven it to bring me cake and balloons. My heart dipped and sank down into my stomach to rest with the nervous bubble-flutters that didn't seem to want to ease up.

I supposed this, at least, answered the question about where Joker had been all night. Though, I wasn't sure why his woman was showing up here at the house I lived in, especially when he wasn't here. I had a fleeting moment of panic thinking she had come to do me harm, but then I straightened my back, making sure my spine was taut as steel before I spoke to the blond woman who had helped ruin my wedding night memories forever. "Can I help you?"

"Hey," the woman breathed out, trying to sound sexy or sultry for some reason. "Is Joker here? He forgot this…" she didn't finish her statement, instead opting to point to a pair of boxer shorts that were hanging out of her purse in plain view.

"You know what?" I asked in my saccharine sweet southern drawl. "He stepped out a minute, but everyone should be here soon. Come on in, sweetheart. Make yourself at home."

I stepped out of the way and even hooked my hand around her arm when her eyes flared in shock. She had been about to turn and bolt, but I wasn't having that. She came here with an agenda, and I was going to make sure she got exactly the level of drama she'd been craving.

"No, really. I insist. To be sure, he's missing those," I told her as I closed the door and had her take a seat in the kitchen. "I'll be right with you," I called out to her before I marched my ass to the place I'd set up the printer for my school work and I printed two pictures off of my phone. Then I smiled at the woman as I moved to the bedroom and went to dig around in my closet. I found the wedding photo frame I'd purchased two years ago. I'd found it in an antique shop and knew that I had to have it for when I got married one day. It was gorgeous and held a spot for two 5x7 photos with an engraved heart in the middle that stated, "Marriage is Sacred, Love Always". I opened it up and hurriedly placed the photos in it, then replaced the backing and took it out to the living room where I set it in pride of place on the middle of the kitchen island right next to the stupid potato salad I'd made for Joker the Jerk.

The girl couldn't see what the frame contained from her seat at the kitchen table, but I noticed her squirming around nervously anyway before I turned a fake smile her way. "I really think I should…" the girl started to say, but was cut off by boisterous laughter as my whole family and Joker piled through the doorway.

"Nonsense," I told her. "Everyone is here now," I threw my arm out toward the people who had all moved into my living room, unaware of what they had just walked in to. Then it happened.

"Oh shit!" I heard murmured.

"Oh shitake mushrooms, indeed!" I sang out sweetly. I had never been one to cuss, and even as spitting mad as I was now, I wouldn't stoop to using that kind of language. I had only done so once before and I'd had instant regrets after the words left my lips. Everyone came to a stop. Some of them appeared puzzled by what was going on. I moved aside so they'd be able to see the photo frame on the counter.

"Look, Joker," I called out. I turned to the girl sitting, ringing her hands at the kitchen table. "Sorry, how rude of me. I didn't get your name, sweetheart."

She looked too stunned to speak, so I waved away the thought. "Never mind," I chirped out in a faux happy voice. "She was here to return your," I glanced back at the woman. "What was it again?" I leaned down and snagged the boxers from her purse, and dangled the waistband from my finger. "Apparently, you left these with her last night."

Every eye in the room except Merc's and Lily's turned accusing looks his way.

"That's a fuckin' lie!" He yelled the words out, thankfully directing his anger toward his whore and not me. I dropped the offensive underwear. "I don't even fuckin' know you!" Joker spat the words in the girl's direction and I watched as she flinched.

"Now, that's a mother truckin' lie if I ever heard one," I stated coolly, forcing his eyes to come back to meet mine. I slid over another step so the wedding photos were in plain sight for him too. "You know her very intimately. You know her so intimately that you consummated our marriage with her on our wedding night. Shoot, you drove her piece of crap car to this house just yesterday to deliver me an ice cream cake and balloons." I felt sick to my stomach at the thought that hers had been the car that he had procured for that task when he mentioned he had gotten it from a hanger on. To think I was going to let him back into my life. I pointed to the wedding photos and left the room.

When I got to the bedroom, I was shaking so hard I had to sit down. The tears fell right around the time the shouting started in the other room. My mom rushed in and shut and locked the bedroom door behind her.

"Oh sweetie, why didn't you just come home? If I had known…"

"No. I have enough money saved for a small apartment now. I'm not coming home, but I can't stay here either. Not now."

"If it helps, the girl lied. He was with Merc and Tiger Lily all night. First helping with club business and then he crashed there so he could pack all of his stuff and bring it home today."

I shook my head. "He still borrowed her car yesterday and brought me gifts in it. Hers, of all the cars in the world? That was insulting."

"I was there when he needed to borrow a car yesterday, honey. I didn't have mine with me or I would have handed him the keys. One of the other men put those keys in his hands. I don't think he knew who the car belonged to."

I swallowed thickly. "That girl is just a symptom of the disease, Momma. We aren't good for one another and I don't think I'm strong enough to be like Tiger Lily and forgive. Our wedding night will always be tainted – even more than the crappy event itself. I felt more like I was being sold off than entering into wedded bliss. I should have just turned and run then. I just kept thinking that he agreed to do it, and maybe it meant there was something there."

"Anna," my mom whispered as she pulled me into her arms.

"I thought I was moving past the hurt and then she showed up today and threw it all back in my face."

"Oh, baby girl."

Chapter 11

When I pulled up to the house, there were several cars and

bikes lining the street, leaving the driveway open for me to pull the truck in. They were all waiting out there for me too, as if afraid to enter the house and ruin the surprise for Anna.

"I told you guys that she already knows you're all coming over," I joked with them.

"You organized this for our baby," Lucy told me. "We didn't want to go in without you. I took hold of the duffle that had been tossed into the back of the truck this morning. It was good to finally be coming home, especially since I felt things finally moving in the right direction with Anna. Talking to her yesterday had been very reminiscent of the times we'd spent together before our happy little couple-bubble blew up and I found out she was the VP's daughter. She was his youngest, under-age daughter to be exact. Granted, by law, she wasn't underage, but in the club's eyes I could have lost my ability to become a full-fledged member by being with her. If she hadn't lied about a couple things, at the time, I would have said she was worth losing the club over. I couldn't contain the smile that spread across my face as I moved closer to these people. Since I was discharged from the Army they had become my family. Knowing that they were going to more of a family as Anna and I grew closer again was only a bonus.

"You look like a new man today," Merc commented.

"It feels great to finally be heading in the right direction again," I answered.

"'Bout time," Double-D grumbled.

"Now, don't fuck it up!" Ever scolded playfully as we walked through the door. Her blunt reply had everyone laughing as we did so.

We all managed to file through the door and into the living room when my eyes met Anna's. She was smiling, but her smile didn't reach her eyes. Something was very wrong. It dawned on me then that I hadn't let her know I wouldn't be back last night, but it should be easily cleared up since Merc and Lily were here to vouch for me. That's about the time I heard another voice.

"I really think I should…" the woman sounded panicked as she got ready to stand, but my wife interrupted her.

"Nonsense, everyone is here now."

An exchange of lowered voices happened, but I couldn't make out what they were saying before Anna turned our way again. She turned my way specifically.

"Look, Joker," she started before turning back to the curvy little blond dressed like she was going clubbing rather than a family birthday party who also seemed absolutely terrified now. "Sorry, how rude of me," Anna was saying with mock sweetness. "I didn't get your name." She paused, but seemed to think better of allowing the woman to speak. "Never mind," she turned her attention back to me then. "She was here to return your…" Her head swiveled back to the as yet named woman again. "What was it again?" She bent awkwardly, squishing her adorable, yet still smallish, baby bump as she did. The she retrieved men's underwear from the woman's purse. Oh fuck no! I was already seeing where this was going. Anna held them out, dangling them off of a single finger. "Apparently, you left these with her last night."

Every set of eyes in the house moved to me. Most of them not in a kind way. The lying bitch was pleading with her eyes for me to save her from this scene while most the others clearly had my murder on their minds. Everyone except Merc and Lily who knew, without a doubt, it wasn't true.

"That's a fuckin' lie!" The words flew from my mouth laced with both truth and accusation. Anna dropped the underwear to the floor, but I turned to the blond. "I don't even fuckin' know you!" I yelled at her.

"Now, that's a mother truckin' lie if I ever heard one," Anna started with only a tiny bit of cool emotion filtering through her words. "You know her very intimately. You know her so intimately that you consummated our marriage with her on our wedding night. Shoot, you drove her piece of crap car to this house just yesterday to deliver me an ice cream cake and balloons." Oh fuck no! Please, if there is a God out there, tell me that wasn't true. I had taken those keys from a man, not a woman. I glanced at the woman in question again as Anna shifted and moved over a bit. I didn't recognize her at all. Then again, I'd been completely hammered and thought she was Anna when I'd woken up to her draped over top of me after my wedding night.

When I shifted my glance back to Anna I noticed she had been blocking a new addition to the décor of the house with her body previously. There was an awesome, handcrafted photo frame sitting there. It looked to be silver, or maybe pewter. I couldn't tell from this distance. There was a heart in the middle with words etched into it. I couldn't make out the words from the distance, but I did notice the two pictures that took up space in the frame. They were from our wedding day and night. One was of Anna and me at the courthouse. You couldn't see either of our faces because I had shifted so Anna could only be seen in profile and my hand was held in front of me so my face was obscured from the shot. It was proof of the asshole I had been on our wedding day. I wouldn't even let her sister take a picture of us to commemorate the occasion. It was no wonder she hated me, and couldn't move past my stupid reactions that day.

Nope. Scratch that. I moved from that picture to the one that made me want to puke. Jesus. She had a picture of that? I turned my attention back to the blond woman – the same one who was still sitting shell-shocked at our kitchen table. In the picture, she had been going down on me. It had clearly been the same night I got married to Anna. The most damning part of it was I looked to be seriously enjoying it in that picture. I didn't even fucking remember it happening, let alone who it had happened with. When I was finally able to tear my eyes away, it was to see that Anna had fled the room. I turned my glare on the woman from the picture, but I focused on the version of her still seated at my table.

"You gave this to her today?" I roughly questioned the woman sitting there.

"Oh my God!" The woman shrieked as she finally turned to

see what I had been staring at. "Who took that? Why would someone take a picture of that?" She seemed genuinely upset at the idea that someone had taken the picture, which led me to believe that she hadn't been the one to give it to Anna. That begged the question, where did it come from then? Surely, she hadn't taken it herself. Merc had told me he took her out of there when I was just kissing another woman. Apparently, that had been the blond woman sitting in front of me too.

"I didn't know you had gotten married that day. You didn't even speak to her at all that night. I thought she was just another club slut wanna-be, or I swear I would have never come here." Tears streamed down her face. "I'm so ashamed. She's pregnant. I didn't know she was pregnant either. What kind of a horrible person do I look like now?" The woman was babbling and blubbering as she spoke. "You borrowed my car yesterday, and I thought it meant something. I thought you finally remembered our night together, and…" She cried some more. "When I got here and saw her, I figured she was just a club slut. It turns out I'm the homewrecking slut. How could you do that to such a sweet girl? She couldn't even cuss at you after what you did. Oh my God! After what I did with you!" She glanced over to Merc and Double-D then. "I'm so sorry. I didn't know. I swear!" She knew her ability to show up at the clubhouse would be nil with the admission that she had come here to find me and decided to cause trouble when she found another woman in my house instead. The club had a zero tolerance policy with that type of drama since Toby had been killed by a crazy, jealous club whore.

"Get out of my house," I hissed at her. She wasted no time doing just that. I noticed Deck followed her to the door saying something as they went and causing her crying jag to ramp up. I had moved without thought to the kitchen island where the photo frame sat mocking me with the worst mistakes I'd ever made. I snatched it up ready to launch it across the room when Ever was suddenly there yanking it out of my hand.

"Don't you dare!" She took the back off the frame and tore the pictures out then tossed them to the floor like they were on fire. Then she reverently put the frame down on the counter. "She bought that years ago to save it for her wedding photos because it was perfect in her eyes." Ever teared up while talking about it. "I remember hearing Momma-Luce tell her she was too young to worry about stuff like that. Anna insisted she'd regret it forever if she didn't get it then, because she'd never find another one like it. She insisted her wedding photos had to go in it one day."

I hadn't allowed Anna to have a single usable photo of our wedding. Now, the damn frame was tainted by the horrible memories I'd left her with of a day that was supposed to be sacred. Never in my life had I thought of harming myself for any reason, but in that moment I finally understood the amount of despair and self-loathing necessary to contemplate doing just that. As it turned out, I didn't need to worry about inflicting harm on myself. Before I could even register the movement, Ever had hauled off and clocked me right in the corner where my eye and nose met. I actually stumbled back from the impact, having been caught by surprise at her attack.

"That's my girl!" Double-D called out. He must have been ready to pounce too, but when I turned to take the much deserved hit from him, Merc had a hold of him instead.

"He was with me and Tiger Lily every night since they split up, last night included."

"That picture, those pictures," Double-D pointed to the offending things lying on the floor. "That was my baby girl's wedding night!"

"I know," I offered up miserably. I grabbed the pictures and started ripping at them furiously, not even realizing I was crying like a baby in front of everyone.

"She can never unsee that," Lily informed me, breaking the silence that had descended over everyone else there. "But honey, she had that picture since her wedding night."

I glanced up at Lily through eyes swimming with tears and my face crumpled with more emotion than I could handle. "She knew? All this time?"

"Why do you think she avoided you at all costs before?" Ever asked, though she seemed just as shocked about the fact that her sister had known all along as the rest of us.

"Makes sense now, especially her panicked rant about not wanting STDs from you." I was thankful Ever didn't repeat Anna's worries about me raping her. I didn't think I'd survive that considering present company.

I stood, moving toe to toe with Double-D, and looked him in his eyes as I spoke. "Take her away from me. I've done nothing but hurt her and I can't…" I choked up and had to start over. "I can't do this to her anymore. I fucked it all up from the beginning. There's no going back now."

"Do you love my daughter?" He asked just as quietly as I had spoken.

"Yes, that's why you have to do this," I pleaded with him. He nodded his head once and walked toward the direction of the bedroom where Lucy had gone to be with her daughter.

"D?" Merc called out.

"You should go on home now," Double-D answered. "Pretty sure baby girl is fresh out of things to celebrate today."

Misery swam in my stomach as his words just reiterated how badly I had fucked everything up. I tried to make sure her birthday was one that she would remember. She would definitely never forget this one, and that was the kicker. I'd do anything to wipe this memory away and give her a fresh, clean slate. I couldn't though, because one angry night of being fucked up and drunk off my ass had left us in a state of disrepair with ripple effects that were still hitting hard every time we let our guards down around one another. It was like some force beyond the grave was trying to keep us apart. For a moment, I thought maybe it was Toby, himself. Then I figured there was no way he would put his little sister through this, even if he wanted to spite the man he didn't think was good enough for his sister.

I sat on the stool at the kitchen island and allowed my head to sink into my hands while my elbows propped it up. I felt a pat on my back before Merc and Tiger Lily took off and then Deck and Ever were there. "I know you don't want to hear this right now, but remember when you told me she was better off not knowing how far things went with you and the blond that night?" Ever asked.

"Yeah," I mumbled without lifting my head.

She made a noise in the back of her throat and then started talking again. "She deserved to hear it from you. Part of what has had her on edge has been her inability to trust what you were up to when you weren't around. I know that despite being married, you guys aren't really together like that, but she's pregnant with your kid. Of course she would think about how many other women you're with since she knows you aren't doing anything with her. Knowing what happened that night probably made all of her fears, and the things she made up in her head every time you were gone, seem real. I'm just guessing here, but I bet if you had come clean in the beginning she would have trusted your word about what you've been up to, and she would have known that woman was lying today."

I never bothered to lift my head or acknowledge Ever. I listened as she moved away and pushed out of the door. "I'm pretty sure my wife just helped to open that wound in your gut a little wider. She's not wrong in what she said either, but I want you to hear something else and let it sink in. That girl in there just asked you to move back in so you could work on a relationship again – whether as friends or more down the road – and she did that knowing the truth even if you weren't the one to tell it to her. Remember that. Having that bitch show up here today made everything fresh in Anna's mind again, but give her time, and you'll get back on track again."

I wished I could believe that. I wished I could believe that my supreme fuck up hadn't cost me the mother of my child, and hell, at this point probably my child too. I had just managed to get her to agree to let me in enough to be a part of the pregnancy with her. Holding her belly the day before had left me feeling raw and hopeful all at once. Now, all of that was gone again. The blink of an eye never meant as much as the moment when I happily walked into my home, only to watch everything crash and burn around me again.

"Luce?" I heard Double-D call out from the hallway once he realized the bedroom door had been locked. I turned to tell Deck I had a key to the room, but both he and Ever were gone already. They must have slipped out just after Merc while I was lost in my thoughts and grief. The imposing figure of my father-n-law moved inside the room once the door was opened, and all I could think was that they were going to take her away from me and I deserved it. I had made this happen with my own actions. I had fucked up something that would have been the best thing in my whole fucking life, and I did it because I couldn't get over a simple goddam lie in the big scheme of things.

I wasn't sure how Deck imagined his sister-in-law could possibly get over what I had done, considering the fact that I had gone off the rails over something that was a tiny offense in comparison to what I had done. My stomach rolled with the self-loathing and the regret I was swimming in. I hated that too, deep down, because I had never been a person to look back and dwell before. Neither had I been the type of person who would take things sitting down without a fight. The problem was, I didn't know if fighting for her would make everything better or worse for Anna in the end. The last thing I wanted to do was cause her any more pain than I already had.

Whispered voices caught my attention as I watched Lucy leave the bedroom, avoiding looking in my direction as she marched straight out my front door without so much as a word. She didn't seem happy about having to go either. Double-D came out next, but unlike his wife, he didn't avoid me. Instead, he came straight over to me and made sure I was looking him in the eye as he spoke.

"You have one week, and then I help her get an apartment, and if you're lucky, it won't be one half way around the world." Double-D didn't wait for an answer. He turned on his heel and left my house, thudding the door shut behind him as he went. It took me a minute to realize what had just happened. They had left without her. She was still here. Fuck me, if I knew why, but I would do whatever it took to make her see that things would be different.

I waited for her to come to me, because I didn't think she would appreciate me making the gesture when it was me who she was angry with. It took less time than I'd expected though, and I ached all over again when I saw her face was puffy from crying and her eyes were swollen and red. Not for the first time, I wanted to bring that bitch – whoever the hell the blonde had been – back and punch her in the face for causing Anna's pain. I wanted to punch the shit out of myself too. Anna took one look at me then turned around and headed toward the freezer. She came back with a bag of frozen peas and handed them to me. I just stared at her for a minute wondering what that was all about when she smiled.

"Whoever hit you did a good job. You should put that on your face before you have any more swelling." I had almost forgotten about the hit Ever had gotten in on my face. The pain had never registered, but I figured that was because I had stronger aches going on inside.

"Your sister packs a hell of a punch for such a little thing," I told her. She grinned at that. It was brief, but fantastic to see until the grin faded to a sorrowful glare.

"That was embarrassing," she admitted. "It would have been something else altogether if my entire family hadn't been here to witness and hear that my husband hated me so much that he cheated on me on our wedding night, and that he didn't even care I was sitting there watching him do it."

"You were there for that?" I asked, puzzled.

"I was there for enough, but since you never even knew I had gone, I assumed it wouldn't have mattered to you."

"It matters. I didn't even know. The next day, when I was told about it…"

She eyed me skeptically. "You had to be told about it?"

"I did. When Deck came by the clubhouse, he had to wake me up and there was a woman lying on me. I thought it was you."

"Last I checked, I'm not a blond."

"It took me a while to be able to prise my eyes open. I drank more that night than I've ever consumed before in my life. I'm surprised I didn't need to go to the hospital."

"I get that you're trying to explain away not knowing you had the wrong woman lying with you, but here are my issues with that." She held up her hand and then ticked up one finger first. "The fact that you had to get that drunk because you married

174

me. I have to say, that hurts a lot." She shook her head when I started to speak. "No, it's my turn. You just listen for a minute."

Then she ticked up another finger, now holding two in the air. "The second thing is that you may have been too drunk to know who you woke up with, but when we first got to the clubhouse you hadn't even bottomed out your first drink when a woman was hanging all over you as I watched. That same woman came and stood beside me as she ordered your next round of drinks for the both of you. She even smiled at me before going back to you, handing you your beer, and brushing her body all over you.

"You weren't even on your third drink by the time a different woman was hanging onto you like she owned your body, and you didn't mind one bit. Again, I had front row seats for that. I also had a prospect serving me Sprite or waters and begging me to let him call someone to come get me. The pity in his eyes when he glanced from the scene you were making back to me hurt so much. I kind of wanted to die that night. I didn't though. I stuck around, because I had nowhere else to go. I couldn't even call a cab to take me to your house because I didn't know where it was or have a key to get in.

"You had a few shots and some more beers before the blond girl who was here earlier started pawing at you, only this time you didn't just tolerate it. You pawed back, you danced with her, you made out with her and you did it all in front of me." Her third finger had gone in the air on that one. "The worst part of that was, I don't think you were doing it to hurt me, because you didn't even know I was there. You should have since you drove me there, but it was like on the way from the courthouse to the clubhouse you had managed to make me disappear in your mind, and by the time you walked through the club house doors I no longer existed for you."

"When you started kissing that woman was about the time Merc came out of his office, saw what was going on, and took me home. I'm not sure how long after I left that you waited to let her suck your dick. I don't think you would have cared if I had been there, but like I said, I also don't think you realized I was." She shrugged her shoulders, speculating again about my frame of mind that night. "You left me in your truck when we got there, and I guess you thought I'd stay like a good dog so you could go in and have your guilt-free fun."

"Anna," I hissed out her name on a ragged breath. "I promise, it wasn't like that."

"It doesn't matter what it was like for you. You weren't the one being treated worse than an unwanted dog. You were the one making me feel less than the scum beneath your shoes while you reluctantly married me. You were the one who left me in the car while you went in to get drunk. You were the one who forgot all about me. And you were the one who had other women all over you, kissing you, blowing you, and waking up with you apparently. So no telling what else happened in between."

"Nothing else happened," I tried to assure her.

"How would you know if you don't even remember the blow job or anything else from that night?"

"Trust me, you don't want the details, but I know." How could I tell her that I still had a lipstick ringing my dick and that it would have been gone if I'd had sex? There was also the fact that the club had video of what went down. It had been erased since then, but I'd seen it so I knew what my night consisted of. Once again, I found myself wishing I could kick my own ass.

She scrunched her nose up at me then and shook her head as if to get rid of the memories, or the thoughts, I'd just put in her head. "My point was, it's embarrassing for me. It was bad enough watching that happen, and then having someone send me a picture of the rest on the day I married you, but to have my family witness the woman coming back and knocking on the door for more?" She grabbed hold of her stomach as if it were bothering her. I wondered, and not for the first time, if all of this stress was harming our baby. That was part of the reason I asked Double-D to take her out of here.

"Are you okay? Is the baby okay?" I asked worriedly when she glanced down at her belly with a funny look on her face. Then she started laughing. What the hell?

Once she got herself under control she explained. "All day

177

long I've been feeling this weird fluttering, bubbly feeling in my stomach. It gets worse when you talk."

"I'm sorry, I'll stop." If you ever want to feel completely dejected just talk to a pregnant woman who is mad at you. Apparently, they don't pull any punches.

"No," she giggled, grinning down at her belly again. "I just realized what it is. I thought it was nerves at first, but it's not. The baby must like to hear your voice because I'm pretty sure that's what I'm feeling. It's moving. I've been getting that feeling on and off for a couple weeks, but I didn't realize…" She grinned up at me. "I thought it was just nerves or something else."

I froze momentarily as I realized what she was saying. The baby was moving inside of her. Our baby. She could feel it moving. My eyes locked on to her stomach and before I knew it I was across the room and sitting on my knees at her feet. "Can I feel?"

"Probably not," she stated as she continued smiling at her belly and mostly ignoring my presence.

"Oh." Well, that was a kick in the balls.

"No, I meant that I don't think you can actually feel it yet. It's just a small fluttering inside me. I can't feel it with my hands. That will be a little bit longer." She must have seen the forlorn look on my face because she scooped my hands up and placed them on her belly. "You can try, but I can't guarantee the results."

I glanced up at her while my hands were wrapped around her small baby bump. The fact that she had just listed off the ways I'd embarrassed and humiliated her on our wedding day, and then turned around and offered me this opportunity astounded me. I hadn't given her even half the consideration she had handed me. She was proving, once more, that the woman was really too good for me in every way.

"Remember when you called me Lise and I called you Evan?"

"Yeah," I responded quietly wondering where she was going with that.

"You know what I loved the most about that?" I turned my head slowly from side to side indicating that I did not know. "I talked, you listened. You really and truly heard what I had to say. When you spoke, I gave that back to you in return. Aside from me using a different nickname for my name it was all beautiful truth and I think you were the first person who ever really understood me and knew what I was all about."

"I felt the same. Everything clicked into place when we used to talk," I admitted.

"Yeah," she mumbled sadly. "That's our problem."

"What that we clicked together?" I asked, confused.

"No. Our problem is that we don't anymore." Not gonna lie. That sucked to hear from her. "We can't," she continued talking.

"When you got angry with me we stopped talking and despite signing our names on paper vowing to do better we never started talking to one another again. So, no click. Just confusion, sadness," she looked me right in the eye before adding the last. "And pain."

I took a moment to process what she was trying to tell me. It was understandable that we stopped talking considering how betrayed I felt by her lies. They had almost cost me everything. Hell, I wasn't even sure she was telling me she wanted to start talking. Not for the first time, I wanted to just hop on my bike and ride out because I couldn't understand what she wanted from me. The problem was, I knew I'd regret the minute I did that because life without Anna was misery and I already knew that for a fact.

Chapter 12

ANNA

"So, are you proposing that we start talking again or that

we stop altogether?" Joker asked warily. I couldn't hide my smile at the hint of insecurity he showed with that question.

"We need to start talking. As much as I was ready to walk out of here with my parents today, I couldn't."

"Do you mind if I ask why? Fuck knows, I don't deserve for you to stay, but if they're forcing you to, I'll…"

The idea was absurd so I waved it off with the flick of my wrist before he even finished. My mom had been tempted to have my father take me from the house against my will, but he had explained how that would go over about as well as a lead balloon. "It's not like that. Actually, something Ever said not so long ago came back to me when I was talking to my mom. The bottom line is that we have to be able to communicate with one another. We have to be able to forgive the things we've done to hurt each other and to move past them without drowning in the misery we've created. I don't want to see my child grow to hate either, or both, of us because we continued to hurt each other and our child as a result. So, we need to talk this out and get past the bad stuff so we can move on to becoming two adults who can speak to one another without flinging mud at each turn."

"When did you become the adult in this relationship?" He teased.

"Yesterday, by law," I answered cheekily, making him laugh.

"Anna, about earlier," he started by I shook my head.

"Don't. There's no need. Today was a good example about why we need to communicate better. Not being open and honest and getting everything off of our chests when it happens just makes it all a festering wound. It doesn't take much to pull at the seams and split the wound wide open again." He simply sat, watching me when I was done speaking, looking for his moment to chime in if I was done. I wasn't. I needed to clarify about the events of the day.

"The picture, and what it represented were things that I had sitting around festering inside of me. If we had talked about it, and been honest about what happened, what you had been up to since, and all the in between stuff, that woman popping up here today would have been a tiny blip on our radar. Hell, you might not have known she was here until after everyone left, because I could have sent her away from the beginning by asking what she wanted with my husband.

"The thing is, I didn't send her away because she opened that wound, and all I had left was to go on the attack. If I'm being honest, I didn't know whether to believe her or not. I had already been struggling with why, after you said you would come and move back in, you never showed up last night and left no word either. I sat here for the longest time trying to stay awake until you got back, but then I couldn't anymore." When I said nothing else, he grimaced and then stood to move toward the kitchen to grab himself a beer and me a bottle of water.

Waiting for him to sit back down was like torture because he just stood, pacing back and forth for a few minutes. Maybe he was trying to decide how much he could tell me, or if I really meant it when I said I wanted us to be open and honest with one another.

"I should have told you immediately, but I honestly thought I was sparing you. Truthfully, I was deeply ashamed of myself when I realized what I'd done. Having you hurt worse by my actions wasn't something I wanted. I can see where I went wrong with not telling you though."

"Don't ever try to spare me. Besides, you never know what I might already have seen or been told."

"Speaking of that," he stated as he came back to stand in front of me. There was a menacing edge to his stance, though I could tell it wasn't aimed at me. At least, I hoped it wasn't. "I don't supposed you'd be willing to let me know who has been filming and spreading around club business?"

"My father knows. He asked the same question and he's dealing with it."

Surprisingly, Joker nodded and left it alone. "What you saw in that picture was all that happened besides her passing out on me later. I swear, nothing else happened. When I was sober enough to realize it wasn't you lying with me, and that no one knew where you were I checked the cameras in the clubhouse. I know exactly what happened that night. I just don't know from first hand memories, only the fast-forwarded images that played out on the security tape. Since that incident there's been no one. Hell, there was no one before that since I found out about the baby."

My jaw probably hit the floor at that revelation. I couldn't wrap my head around that at all. "Why?"

"I know I made an ass out of myself on our wedding day and I fucked up bigger at the clubhouse, but when I said I'd marry you, I meant it in every way. I didn't think it would be just a convenience. I told myself it was, or tried to, but deep down…" he shook his head and couldn't hide the trace of a smile on his lips. "Every time I closed my eyes, I pictured what it would be like to live with you, to hold you again. I saw you in my dreams all swollen with my baby, and even so far as holding our baby one day. Granted, I was still angry and working through things, but deep down I was ready to start a family with you too. I just needed time to figure out how to get past what I saw as a betrayal. I never would have thought myself capable of completely obliterating that feeling and going above and beyond in retaliation, but it seems like that was what I did.

"At any rate, I planned to remain true to our vows in case things worked out, and if they didn't, I could stand on my high horse and tell everyone about how hard I tried." He huffed out a miserable excuse for a laugh then. It didn't convey any humor, simply frustration with himself for the way he had been thinking in the beginning. "Anna, I don't know what the fuck happened in my head that day. Everything got so twisted up and my anger reached its peak."

I understood that. Even if I wished that I didn't.

"I think that's where it would have been beneficial for us to actually speak to one another before we showed up at the courthouse. I didn't think you'd be faithful to me considering the circumstances of our marriage, but I never thought you'd treat me with so much disrespect and hatefulness. It was all a symptom of that open, festering wound. You were like a hurt animal lashing out against those who try to help it. I'm guessing you lashed out at me because I'm the one who hurt you and made you feel caged as a result."

"You ever think about going into the therapy business?" He asked in all seriousness.

"No. I want to be a writer so I can make sure my characters all walk away with their happily ever after."

"Not everyone gets a smooth ride in life," he argued.

"No, but I'd like to think they can overcome the obstacles to find happiness. If they can't do that in my fictional worlds, what hope do I have of ever being happy myself one day?"

I could see that my own personal truth hurt him in some way, but I wouldn't lie about how I was feeling anymore. Not to him, or anyone else, because that particular lie cost me too much already.

"Were you with anyone else while we were apart?"

I laughed at that. "Are you kidding? Who wants to date the girl who's knocked up?"

He raised a brow at me. "Too many men and boys would gladly do it because they'd think they can get in there without protection since you can't be pregnant twice at the same time."

"Well, that's not exactly true. There have been cases where…" I started to tell him, getting off track. He stopped me though.

"Anna, I'm sure that's all very interesting, but it doesn't answer the question."

"The answer is no. I haven't been with anyone else or even thought of doing it." The instant relief on his face made me want to punch the crap out of him. "I was too heartbroken to even notice other people at first," I told him, quickly wiping the smirk off of his face because he knew he couldn't say the same thing since he was already with another woman when I found out I was pregnant. "Then, I started getting sick and had more important things on my mind anyway. Plus, after I was married, there was no way I would break those vows I made since I'd already made such a huge mistake by stretching the truth to begin with." The smirk was completely gone and he was sitting there looking as miserable as I felt inside. Okay, well, being able to talk without slashing wounds open would obviously have to be a work in progress for a while.

"Sorry," I finally managed to get out. "You smirking about it made me angry."

"You have every right to be, Anna. We both handled things in very different ways, and of the two of us, your way was the healthier one. Don't feel bad about putting me in my place when I need it."

"Fine, then I suggest you clean up the party stuff that was never used, since everything got derailed."

"I think I have a better idea."

Chapter 13

"I will gladly clean up, but first I need to ask you something

else," I told her. Her lack of response beyond a nod prompted

me to continue on with the question. "When is your lunch break

at work on Monday?"

"Lunch is anytime I want to take it, so long as we aren't

swamped at the shop. Beth is super lenient and nice about

things. I guess she figured since I was pregnant, things might be

up in the air about when I got hungry or needed a break."

"That's good that she's been that way with you," I told her.

THE PRINCESS *and the* PROSPECT

It still didn't sit right with me that she was working at all while pregnant, but as my old first shirt used to tell me in the Army, I needed to learn to choose my battles and when to fight them. Today wasn't that day. Besides, it got Anna out of the house, wasn't strenuous, and she genuinely seemed to enjoy going to work and hanging out with Beth and Gretchen when she was there instead of the tattoo studio.

"How about you call me just before you're going to take it so I can meet up with you and we can get lunch together?" Seeing the question in her eyes, I didn't wait for her to ask it before adding the reason. "I won't be around tomorrow. I have to go on a run for the club down to Jacksonville tomorrow. I most likely won't get in until late, if at all, depending on how things go. Crow and Kane are probably coming with me. J-Bird was supposed to be the one to take this run, but he's been mostly AWOL since…" I left off the last part, because she already knew where I was going with that. J-Bird had gone off the rails a bit after T-Bone's death, and he hadn't really come back around since.

"I wonder if he's going to be okay?" I could see the sadness in her eyes. Both T-Bone and J-Bird had been brothers to her, even if only one had been by blood. It had to hurt to basically lose them both at once. The only saving grace was that one of them might come back if he ever got past the hurt of losing his best friend and brother.

"He's still grieving. Things will work out, and he'll come home."

"What if he hates the club now?"

"I know for a fact that isn't true. We keep tabs on him. He's been running with Phoenix."

"Phoenix?"

"He's a nomad in the club. The man was on the road for a while with a band before they broke up, so he took nomad status in order to accommodate the club and the band. I think he enjoys the road too much to come back off of it though."

"I wonder why I never met him," she murmured just loud enough for me to hear. She didn't miss the smirk I made at that comment either.

"He's a good looking mother fucker in a rock band, and he's a part of the MC. I wonder why your dad never wanted to introduce him to either of his girls?"

She giggled then. "I guess I see your point. Is he a good guy though? Will Jay be all right with him?"

"I bet money that the guys in the club have seen to it that Phoenix didn't happen upon him by accident, if that makes you feel better."

"Good, I don't think I could stand to lose another brother."

"So, no objections to me going to Jacksonville?" I asked since she had gotten off track when I mentioned J-Bird.

"Um, no. It's club business, so it's not like it matters what I think anyway."

"It matters," I told her.

"Well, I'm okay with you having to do your part for the club. At least I know where you're off to and how long. Some women don't get told that much."

"When it comes to the club, you know I can't tell you everything, but I will always try to tell you everything you need to know. I promise you that, beautiful."

"Thanks," she said softly as a blush stole across her cheeks. It happened every time I called her beautiful, and it never got old seeing how I affected her.

"You're okay with lunch Monday too, right?"

"Yes, I said I was."

"You didn't. That's why I was clarifying." She rolled her eyes at me, which I let go this time. It was good to see her playful, sassy side coming back out. I had missed that about our time together before everything went to shit.

"I guess I can have lunch with you."

"Well, thanks for sounding so eager." As if her stomach read my mind, I heard an almighty growl come from her body. She nervously giggled as she clutched her belly.

"I guess the potato salad sampling earlier wasn't enough," she admitted.

"Did you by chance make that before or after the special guest who ruined the day arrived?"

"Before, why?"

"Just wondering if it's safe to eat or not. If it is, I'll throw some hamburgers and hot dogs on the grill for us. I'm starving, and it sounds like you are too."

"That sounds fine, but I'll pass on the potato salad this time."

I looked longingly at the aforementioned dish knowing I wouldn't eat any if she didn't. She noticed and laughed.

"For heaven's sake, Joker," she called out in an exasperated tone. "It's not like I poisoned the food. I just taste tested a lot of it before company arrived and it soured on my stomach as a result. Just smelling it right now would probably send me to the bathroom." She wrinkled her nose, as if she was already smelling it.

I knew she didn't mean anything by it, but my heart hurt knowing I managed to ruin her birthday celebration with her family – even if it had been inadvertently. Plus, she wasn't even able to eat the food she had prepared.

"Evan," I corrected her use of my road name instead of my given name. I needed to at least fix one thing today, and I might as well start there.

"What?"

"You're still calling me Joker. I thought we worked better using our given names?"

"Oh, I guess so. Your name changed since then and mine was never really…"

It was my turn to wave her words and thoughts away like she normally did to me. "Evan and Anna works for me."

"Evan and Anna," she replied in her delicate voice. I had to turn and get busy making us food then, otherwise I wasn't so sure I could keep my hands to myself for the rest of the evening.

I rolled off the couch when the alarm on my cell phone buzzed me awake. Leaving at 4:30 am had been a shit plan. It was one that might just have Crow eating gravel today. Damn the bastard. I groggily made my way to the hall bathroom, cleaned up, relieved myself, and got dressed in record time. Before I was about to head out, I turned back to the bedroom and opened the door. Anna was there on the bed, fast asleep with her dark hair spilled haphazardly across the pillows. Even in her sleep, she held her belly cradled in her arms as if she needed to protect the child growing there from the world.

I may have been mad about our situation in the beginning, but I was pretty sure Anna was going to end up making a wonderful mother for our children. Shit! What I was thinking? Children? We weren't even at the kissing stage again yet, let alone at a point where I needed to concern myself with getting her pregnant again. Still, that glow in her skin, the twinkle in her eyes when she talked about the baby, and the way pregnancy had filled out her subtle curves had made her one of the most gorgeous women I'd ever laid my eyes on. Actually, there was no competition from anyone I could think of. She was it. I just hoped I would be able to convince her that my fuck up was truly a one-time deal. There was no way in hell I would ever jeopardize losing her again. I Couldn't. There was no way I could survive her going missing from my life again.

Against my better judgement, I moved into the room and kneeled down beside the bed. Without thought, my fingers traced over the silky strands of hair on the pillow before I leaned in a placed a gentle kiss on her forehead. "See you later, beautiful," I whispered. Then I got up and left the room before I managed to call my loyalty to the club in question by staying behind to hold her in my bed. That was another goal I needed to set. The two of us sleeping apart sucked. Even if she wasn't ready for sex just yet, I didn't think I could manage to go too much longer with curling up to her at night.

By the time I got outside, Kane and Crow were both sitting at the end of the driveway waiting on me. "It's about fucking time, Army boy. Didn't they teach you shit about being on time in the military?"

"They taught me a whole fuck of a lot about how to hurry up and wait. You just did that part on your own this morning," I called out to him as Kane chuckled. It didn't take long to get myself situated and the three of us were on the road headed to Jacksonville. Not too long ago, I would have been excited for the trip, and the prospect of branching our club out. When it had first been talked about freely in front of me, I just knew I might jump at the chance to head to Florida if they needed bodies for the new chapter. Now, they couldn't drag me away from this town. My heart was here, and right now it was beating for two. There was no way I'd even think about dragging Anna away from the rest of her family, and even if things didn't work out, I wasn't going to put her through a long-distance custody issue either. That meant staying put. Luckily for me, this was supposed to be a quick run to see if the new location was feasible and to help out some members in the Tallahassee Chapter. Their Prez had gotten in some deep shit while protecting his old lady, and now they were on the ropes for running guns up and down the east coast and a few centralized states on a pipeline directed to and from Canada with pitstops in between.

I wasn't too keen on being a part of that shit, but club was club. We had to support one another, and our mother chapter was behind them for the ten years they managed to get locked into running that shit. They had an escape plan at the end. There was even an emergency plan in case shit went south, but that was a nuclear option that would involve all the chapters. It was also one we weren't able to talk freely about with Kane present. I had no doubts he'd become a member, but the fact of the matter was he was only a prospect at this point.

Hell, truth be told, I wasn't sure why he was even prospecting for the club. From what Deck had told me about all the shit that had gone down with his woman, I wouldn't think Kane would want to be a part of the club. Then again, and I hoped I was wrong, he might have the kind of motivation to join that would eventually get him put to ground. Messing around with another brother's wife and old lady wasn't looked upon too kindly unless that brother and his woman had an open understanding.

We made good enough time on the road to get there in about three and a half hours since traffic was light early on in our journey. We arrived at one of the favored scouted locations and killed the engines. "Looks like we're early and the Florida boys are running a bit behind. They were supposed to get in before we did," Crow commented as he pulled out his cell, presumably to check on the men from our Tallahassee Chapter.

"Damn, since we operate so close to the beach, back home I didn't expect this area to look like the sticks. Why this place?" Kane asked as we both glanced around.

I shrugged my shoulder. "Don't know. From what I understand this is the favored spot."

"Nah, we're at the Old Kings Road property," Crow told whoever he was speaking to, and then he hung up. "Idiots went to the second one on the list. I guess they had some reason to think this place sold already." Crow glanced around. "You want to know why we want this place? Over 20,000 square feet plus a separate office offering another 1,000. Then there's the two coolers that are each 3,000 square feet." He waggled his brows about that. If ever there was a built in space adequate to be used as a torture and kill room, an industrial freezer space would do it. It was already nearly soundproofed, the cool temperatures inside would keep any smell down and preserve whatever might need to be saved, plus it would make for an uncomfortable as hell place to be held prisoner. There were other practical uses for the freezer space too, but since Florida seemed to be a hot bed of bullshit we'd be walking into as a club, it only stood to reason that at least one of them would be used for nefarious purposes.

"There's loading docks and doors, and look at all this glorious concrete," he mentioned after a bit of pause as he threw his hands out to indicate the giant parking area that used to house more than 50 big rig trucks and trailers. This was a shipping company previously and I could definitely see the allure. With very little work, it could become an amazing compound, especially since it already had a barbed-wire fence around the perimeter.

We all glanced up when we heard the pipes in the distance. The Florida boys had arrived.

"Sorry we're late," Crusher stated as he dismounted his bike and came over to greet us. He was the current President of the

Tallahassee Chapter, and a hell of a man. The scar that ran through his right eyebrow was a testament to the fight he put up to keep his woman alive when shit went down with her not too long ago. "I seriously thought Ghost had said this place was off the list."

"Nah, still for sale, and the price just dropped. Something about a vermin infestation on last inspection," Crow offered up with a laugh.

"Sneaky little shit," Crusher applauded.

"Well, God willing, and the creek don't rise, this will be home soon, and I prefer this to the other options. So does the old lady. She has a bit of country in her even though I have her living in the big city of Charleston. If we have to move to sunny Florida, she said she ain't living in the middle of no giant city."

"You're planning to come down?" I asked. I hadn't been privy to every detail of the expansion plan, it seemed.

"Yeah. After the shitstorm I helped cause with Ever, and the fact that I just can't move past the bullshit, we all thought it best I head down here as a senior member for a while."

The fucker still had a hard time being nice to Ever no matter how much everyone pointed out that he had been wrong about the way he had treated her. I was starting to see that maybe Merc and Double-D had been weeding out their problem children in the club slowly, but surely. A brother named PeeWee had been ousted from the club shortly after everything blew up with Ever when it came out that he'd said some pretty heinous things to her, including threats that involved the shit he'd do to her sexually. She had still been underage when he made those threats. He had also been stealing from the coffers over at one of the strip clubs, and no second chances were given. He was stripped of his kutte and all Aces High insignia. Crow apparently wanted a smoother transition away from trouble and had offered to leave when asked. At least he was somewhat intelligent.

"We'll be glad to have you down here, brother," Crusher told him. "We could use some seasoned vets who were around when we were all knee deep in shit and learning to swim with the flies or drown in it."

"Yeah, bunch of these kids now don't know what it means to fly the 1% patch. Aside from dirty club snatch, they've never had a chance to get their hands in it. Especially these green mother fuckers here," Crow taunted.

"No need to," I explained quickly. "Army life taught me all I ever needed to know about how to kill and survive at all costs. What did it teach you?" Crow had been in the military for a short time, but he had been Coast Guard, never served overseas, and was stationed almost solely at a base in northeastern North Carolina until he got out after his first enlistment and moved to Charleston.

"Let's go check this place out," Crow called out, ignoring my question completely. I hated men who bragged about shit when they hadn't been in the heat of anything more than a club whore's pussy – to borrow his own analogy.

The setup wasn't something any club brother could complain about. "Fuck, it's better than what we're currently using back home," Crusher echoed my own thoughts. "There's a lot of building potential here too considering the trucks won't be everywhere."

"It'd probably be a smart idea to get a garage in out by the street side. There's enough room to have the custom ride shop some of the men have been talking about," Crow put in. I just bet he would want that available wherever he ran off to. He was a decent mechanic, but he wasn't custom ride worthy. I wasn't even certain he was trainable beyond what he already knew. Not that he wasn't intelligent enough, just that his own stubborn bullshit would get in his way. That wasn't going to stop him from wanting a larger piece of the club pie that the custom shop would bring in. Profits from club businesses were put into a pool and split amongst the brothers of the club. Officers took a higher percentage, then the rest would be divided equally amongst the rest of the regular members. The men in the chapters where the businesses were earning higher than others were given bonuses based on those higher percentages because they usually worked hands on with those businesses to make them a success.

That was another reason why we were here. Even though the

Tallahassee Chapter had gotten themselves on the hook for the decade of gun-running, that shit was bringing in profit too which meant we all had to do our part to support them since we all saw a piece of the pie.

The men looked over the property more in depth while Kane and I sat out by the roadway keeping watch for anyone who may seem a little too interested in what we were doing. The property wasn't the only reason we were here. On the way back, we would end up pushing Kane's bike into a box truck with some precious cargo and scooting to Charleston where it was going to be picked up. Even though I knew a part of my club pay came from it, I wasn't a fan of running the guns. The last thing I needed was to get pinched for gun running before I could straighten things out with Anna and see our baby born.

"Mind if I ask something?"

Kane's attention moved from the horizon to me and back again before he tipped his chin up. "Ask away."

"Why are you prospecting? I thought you guys over at Permanent Marks hated the club on Ever's behalf."

"She's part of the club despite what happened to her, isn't she?"

"Yeah, she is, but her biological family is club. Her husband is too. It's kind of hard to walk away from that."

He nodded his head once. "Well, Deck made me hopeful the whole club wasn't full of morons who treated little girls poorly," he teased. "Seems I was right about that, and besides you have to admire hardened men who can bow down and admit they're wrong. I enjoy the open road too, and don't exactly fit in with the rest of polite society here in the south. Seems these are my people. At least they are if I get through this bullshit prospecting period. Gotta say, not enjoying that part so much."

"What? Say it ain't so? You don't actually like cleaning up used condoms off the floor after a party or the nasty bathrooms after some of those fuckers explode their guts out?"

"Jesus, what is wrong with that one guy?" I furrowed my brow just as he said, "Tuesdays are the worst."

I laughed then. "You're talking about Grit, and his wife thinks Taco Tuesday is something of a holiday, never to be missed. The rest of us think Grit could do without the bean burritos though. She always sends him to the clubhouse afterward too. Damn near the only night he doesn't stay home with her these days. Three guesses as to why she encourages that."

Kane laughed. "Smart woman."

"You do know the policy about messing around with another brother's woman, right?"

Kane turned a critical eye on me then. "I have no interest in any of the brother's women." We both sat silently contemplating that. "Does that extend past death?" He finally asked.

"I think that depends on the circumstances. No one would

begrudge the woman moving on, and it'd be damn hard for a club woman to move on in a different lifestyle if she's been in it a long time." I shrugged. "I don't think there's any hard or fast rule against it, if that's what you're asking."

"It is."

"You know, knocking a brother off to get his woman wouldn't be looked upon favorably though," I added with a hint of laughter in my voice. Kane threw his back and laughed heartily at that.

"That's good to know too," he grinned at me as the other men finally came outside. "Not that I planned to do that, but just in case you don't get your shit together where Anna is concerned, you might want to think about how some of the younger brothers look at her. Neil hasn't shut up about the night she sat at the bar."

"Neil?"

"One of the other prospects," he informed me. "Though, I don't really see you having to worry about that guy. He's a bit too soft for the life. Surprised he made it this long."

"You sound like you know a little more about club life than you're letting on."

"My Uncle used to run with the Renegades in North Carolina. Any time we'd go up to visit, he also dropped me by their club to get my fill of bikes. Probably helped my sister's case a bit too when she became best friends with Ever. My mom nearly had a fit about her daughter hanging out with that kind of girl, at first. Then she met Ever and fell in love with her. She wishes Ever could have gone to college with Erin. My little sister has been partying and getting into a little trouble over there at USC. I'm going to end up making a trip to Columbia to straighten her ass out before she flunks out of school."

"Well, damn. You're making me thankful I don't have a sister."

"Oh, but you do." I gave him an odd look and he just laughed. "You married into your wife's family, man. That means Ever is your sister, and heaven help you when Deck starts calling for help when Erin comes home and drags Ever into her bullshit." He laughed. "Hell, now that's she's older you better watch out. They're liable to drag Anna into their drama too once she's had your kid."

"You know, Florida is looking like a real nice location to move my family to," I joked as a small cargo truck became visible a couple miles down the road. I lifted my fingers to my lips and let out a whistle to alert the others that we had company. Receiving the whistle back meant it was the shipment we were waiting on. It wasn't long until Crow and Crusher had finally joined the rest of us to wait by the front gate. We loaded up Kane's bike, and just managed to get back on the road before 2 pm.

I sent Anna a text just before we took off.

THE PRINCESS *and the* PROSPECT

Me: Might make it home before 7.

Thanks to a wreck on I-95 coming up towards Savanna, we ended up losing quite a bit of time. Had it just been us on the bikes, we could have easily circumvented the traffic jam. Since Kane was driving the box van, that wasn't possible. As a result, and a delay in our meet to have the van picked up by the other party, I didn't get in until nearly 10:30 pm. Anna had already been asleep when I got there, so I didn't bother waking her. Instead, the guest room was where I reluctantly ended up for the night. By the time I woke in the morning Anna was already gone. Not wanting her to think ill of me I sent a text.

Me: Sorry, got in later than I thought thanks to accident on road. Didn't want to wake you last night. Are we still on for lunch?

Anna: Of course.

I waited a few more minutes to see if anything else would come through, but it didn't. I wasn't sure what to make of that. Anna could be angry with me, busy, or just indifferent to whether I came home at all. We had the talk about how I planned to be with only her from here on out unless she decided she no longer wanted to be married to me. Somehow, I wasn't so sure she believed it. I couldn't blame her, and once again, I felt sick to my stomach that I had fucked up so horribly and allowed my anger to lead me down a path I couldn't easily come back from – if at all. God, I hoped things worked out though, because a life without Anna in it would be a miserable existence.

When I couldn't deal with driving myself crazy any longer, I got ready and then headed to the clubhouse for a bit until lunch. There weren't many people up and about there since it was still early, but there was a familiar prospect sweeping the floors, and after what Kane had revealed to me recently, I thought maybe it was time to have a chat with this little prick.

"Prospect!" I called out and his head immediately lifted to glance in my direction. The kid had no poker face at all. He schooled his features quickly, but not soon enough to cover for the disgust I saw there. I fucking deserved it, and I knew I did, but brothers weren't supposed to judge one another, even when we were doing stupid shit. This kid was proving another weakness before he could join the brotherhood.

When the man didn't move, I crooked my finger at him as if he were a child I was calling over to me for a scolding. His lips tightened, but he set aside the broom he had been pushing and made his way to me. "You have a problem with me?"

"No,"

"No?" I asked him. "No, what?"

"No, I don't have a problem with you."

"Seems like you do," I countered. He just stood there, stoic and silent as the day is long. "You got a thing for my wife?" Once again, he couldn't contain the flash of fury that crossed his face before he spat words back at me that stung like a bitch.

"Didn't know you were married considering last time I saw you here, there were multiple women crawling all over your jock," the man answered.

"You lying to a brother?"

"No, I didn't know you were married then. I've since heard whispers that maybe you're with one of Double-D's daughters, but I haven't seen her around since the night I last saw you with all those women."

"You catered to her that night, and were pretty attentive from what I've been told." He shrugged his shoulders at me, a careless move. "Speak freely, Prospect, and get it off your chest now. We'll never speak of it again unless you give me reason to. If you make it to a full patch, I'll even give you one free hit the minute you put it on.

"Worth it just for that then," he muttered. Oh yeah, this guy had a hard-on for my woman. "Fine. Even if I lose my place here, someone needs to speak up. They should have done or said something that night. I was fucking sick for that girl having to watch what she did and I didn't even realize you had gotten married to her that day. I just knew she came here with you and had to wait for you to take her back out. I offered her a ride when she looked like she might be sick watching you get pawed on by all those women. I heard Merc got her out of the place before you fucked around with one of them. That is the only reason I came back here after that night. Someone cared about that girl, and what she was witnessing. I don't want to be a part of a club that purposely torments their women. What you did might not have been physical, but you abused that girl just the same that night."

And that took the wind right the fuck out of my sails, because fuck if he wasn't right. I nodded my head and then tipped it, indicating I wanted him to follow me to the bar. I walked behind it and told him to take a seat. He followed directions, watching me like a hawk, curious eyes never leaving me. "When the time comes, you have my vote."

"What?" He asked shocked as I slid a shot his way.

"I came in here pissed off and ready to fucking throw your ass out of here for daring to think about my woman, but you're right. What I did was the lowest, shittiest thing you could do to a person – especially one carrying your child." The man just sat still, not touching the shot, and waited. "I respect your feelings on the matter. I had my reasons and my anger got the best of me that night. Even though I thought I was justified in getting shitfaced, I never intended for things to get out of hand the way they did.

I swallowed my embarrassment and fessed up to a fucking prospect. "Hell, I had forgotten she was there. I had left her outside in the truck because I needed some space to clear my head so I wouldn't say some nasty shit to her that was brewing in the back of my mind. None of that matters now though. It happened. I'm the fucker who screwed everything up. You took care of my woman when I wasn't enough of a man to do it. Not only that, but you just risked your future patch to come to her defense and call me on my bullshit."

The man slipped the shot back toward me and grinned. "I don't drink."

"What the fuck? How are you prospecting for an MC and you don't fucking drink?" I asked, bewildered.

"Let's just say I learned my lesson and it didn't turn out as well as yours. Don't touch the stuff anymore. I'm prospecting because I like the idea of a brotherhood and I'm on my bike damn near every day of the year anyway." He shrugged his shoulders. "Just made sense to me. Besides, I know I'm not the typical recruit, but I have my attributes that will make me damn useful to the club."

"You earned my vote and a personal marker from me then. The only caveat is that personal doesn't extend to my wife in any way." I let him hear the warning tone in my voice as I said it.

He smirked at me. "I don't want your woman. I just wanted her to not have to deal with you being a jackass and humiliating her in front of your whole club. I thought it was bad when I took her for a hang around. Finding out she's a club princess and your wife just made me see red."

"Okay, Saint, you keep calling it like it is and I think we'll get along. I'm over my fucked up bullshit, but just in case…"

"I have your back then, just in case." He stood and turned to go back to the job he'd been tasked with, but ended up turning back to seek me out over his shoulder. "And I'm no fucking saint," he added.

"You are now," I informed him before heading to the office to seek out Merc.

"What can I do for you?" Merc asked without looking up from what he was staring at on the computer monitor in front of him.

"Wanted to talk to you about the prospect working out there right now."

"Neil? The one you just had a confrontation with?" He asked nonchalantly. I grinned at him as he turned his attention away from the monitors and put the full weight of his stare on me.

"The one I just had a chat with. I'm guessing you didn't have audio running?"

"Nope, should I have?"

"You should probably go back and listen in for a minute."

Merc did just that with his eyes twinkling as he nodded his head in approval. "You wanted that pointed out to me, why?"

"Didn't think he was made for this club, but he just proved me wrong. Wanted you to know that."

THE PRINCESS *and the* PROSPECT

"I already knew that, but you just gave me more reason to like him." I stared at Merc a moment and he didn't miss the puzzled look on my face. "What?"

"I thought he was about to be washed, judging from what Crow was saying on our trip. Even Kane thought the club was going to scrape him off."

"Kane is just a prospect himself, so he don't know shit. As for Crow, he's not much longer for this chapter, and he knows it. I think anyone he can make look worse than him at this point is where he puts his focus, and tries to divert others there as well. Since we removed PeeWee, and there's no longer a worse brother here, he's escalated his bad mouthing of anyone who seems to be an easy target. Saint, as you dubbed him, is not an easy target despite the face he shows those he's testing out. Make no mistake, he's testing our club more than we are testing him."

That was interesting to note, but nothing I could explore in the moment as I felt my phone vibrate. I grinned down at the message. As simple as it was, I felt lucky that she'd even sent the damn thing.

Anna: Ready in 20 minutes.

Me: Be there soon.

"I don't even have to ask who that was judging by the goofy grin on your face." I glanced up at him and saw that he didn't appear to be happy. "I don't want to see her hurt. Not sure how you convinced her to stay, but if you're not serious…"

211

"You knew that bitch was lying. I wasn't ever with her past that one night, and I didn't even remember who the hell she was to begin with. Besides, I didn't convince Anna to stay. I tried to let her go. She stayed anyway. She's fucking smarter than I am so I'm just going to follow her lead," I admitted.

Merc threw his head back and laughed. "Hell, Joker, maybe there's hope for you after all. If I had come to that conclusion sooner, Tiger Lily and I might have been spared some shit we went through. They are always smarter than we are. Never doubt that." I stood, waiting to be dismissed. "I appreciate you coming in and going to bat for Saint, even though you have reason to be wary of the fucker. Just remember that though. You fuck up again, and there's always someone waiting in the wings who will be the shiny new thing that makes you look even worse than you made yourself look."

"Thanks for that, I guess," I hesitantly told him as I slipped another step closer to the door.

Merc laughed again. "Get out of here and tell Anna I said hello and not to be a stranger. Tiger Lily would love to see her soon."

"I'll let her know."

I managed to arrive at the photo studio in less than fifteen minutes. When I got there Anna was working with a customer behind the little counter, showing her some photos that had already been taken. The woman seemed thrilled with whatever she was viewing, and he could see that Anna was in her element. The compliments rolled off her tongue without any hesitation or deception. She meant every word of what she was saying to the woman, and ended up convincing her to go with several options in a larger package than she had originally intended to get. I glanced around at some of the photos proudly displayed on the walls as I waited for them to finish up and an idea struck.

I wasn't ready to present it just yet, but hopefully soon, I would have the perfect plan in place to make sure Anna would be mine for the rest of our lives. I didn't mind working for it. I didn't even mind that I'd have my work cut out for me thanks to my initial fuckups. The truth was, my life wouldn't be the same without her brilliant light shining in it. I was just enough of a selfish prick to want that. Hopefully, I was a smooth enough man to make it happen.

Once Anna was finished, she practically bounced over to me. "Where are we going? I'm starving."

It was only then, as I glanced down at her baby bump and part of the reason she was starving, that I realized I had ridden here on my motorcycle. "You do have the truck here, right?" I asked belatedly, having forgotten that she probably shouldn't be riding on the back of my bike now. She smiled up at me knowingly. "I do, but there are plenty of places right around here in walking distance. Why don't we hit one of them and then maybe these cankles I'm developing will calm the heck down," she insisted while pushing a slim foot forward to show me how her ankles looked slightly puffy.

"Cankles?" I asked just for clarification.

"Yeah, you know, when your ankles get so fat they make it look like your calf ends at your foot?"

I laughed at her then. "I don't think you have anything to worry about," I told her as I wrapped an arm around her still very slender shoulder. "Let's go get you guys something to eat though before the tiger growling in your belly decides I look tasty." I watched as her face flamed red as she playfully slapped at my abs. I'd missed this after we split up before. We used to tease and play around so effortlessly. Made me want to kick myself in the ass all over again for allowing my pride fuck it all up. I brushed the thought away though, determined to be in the present with Anna. She never pulled away as we wandered down the narrow sidewalk. "Gretchen must be paying a mint to rent that space."

"Why do you say that?"

"Look around, we're in the hub of Charleston. Leases on Market St. places aren't exactly cheap."

"I guess, but she does do a lot of business. Plus, she also does weddings and big events too. She's talked about training me to be a photographer too and hiring me on for more of that once the baby is born."

"I thought you wanted to be a writer?" She worried her

hands together nervously before answering.

"I do, but I kind of like the photography too," she admitted.

"It's okay to enjoy more than one thing. It gives you something to fall back on if one or the other isn't bringing in the income or job satisfaction that you want."

"I guess so. Though, I don't think the job satisfaction will matter quite so much as being able to pay the bills."

"You don't ever have to worry about paying the bills, Anna. I have you covered."

"You can't promise that."

"I just did."

"But, what if things don't work out? Don't you think your new woman down the road will have a problem with you paying my bills too?"

"There isn't going to be another woman down the road, Anna. I keep trying to tell you that, and you're not getting it." She gave me a dubious look before turning all of her focus on putting one foot in front of the other.

"We'll see," she murmured before her slight movements turned us toward the Crab House near South Market and State St.

"I thought pregnant women weren't supposed to eat fish or something?" I asked as we were seated.

"Good thing I want the house burger then, huh? Besides, I love the smell of the seafood. If I can't eat it, I should at least be able to smell it, right?"

"I suppose. Isn't that like teasing yourself with what you can't have?"

"I don't know. You tell me?"

"What is that supposed to mean?" I asked, curious as to where she was going with that.

"Having me around and claiming you want only me has to be difficult on you when I refuse to be with you right now." Her voice was low, and beyond that, she also seemed as though she feared the answer. I understood that. I had put that fear there with my own actions, and I was fucked, because there was no taking that away from her now. Only time and rebuilding trust through my actions would help ease it.

"If you're asking how I will manage, I'm going to tell you that I'll be 'just fine'. Anna, I'm not a young boy. I have control of my hormones." At her withering glare, I amended my words. "I was overseas for 13 months on my last tour and celibate the whole time. It's not a difficult thing to do. The promise of having you with me again eventually is sure as fuck better than the promise of coming back home to empty, unfulfilling encounters. You're worth waiting for, beautiful."

She blushed again, as she always did when I called her that. Then she glanced up at me with serious eyes. "What if I can't do it? What if I can't get past everything to go there again?"

"I don't want to dwell on what ifs, Anna. I will say, we'll cross the hurdles as we come to them, but no matter what, my first priority is to see that you are never hurt again, at least not in the ways I've hurt you. I'm sure there will be arguments and fights at some point. I don't think there's a healthy relationship out there without their share. My other priority is to make sure that we can maintain a friendly relationship no matter what, because you're right, we have a child we made together. Ever was right, we don't need to do to our baby what either of her parents ended up doing to her."

She was quiet for so long that the waitress managed to bring us our food and move away again before she spoke. "I want to be able to move past everything. I need you to know that, but I don't want to lie either. I'm not sure that I can. There are things about our wedding day and night that haunt me when I close my eyes. If I knew how to make that stop, I would. I just don't yet. Ever got me an appointment to see her therapist. I went to see her and, while she was okay with taking me on, she suggested that because of our circumstances I might benefit from speaking to someone who could help with us as a couple in conjunction with personal therapy."

"I'll do it," I agreed.

"Just like that?"

"Just like that. No question. I wish we had been in a place in the beginning to do just that instead of letting hurt feelings and mostly misplaced anger rule actions."

"Okay," she hummed out before popping a French fry in her mouth. "I'll set something up and let you know."

"You do that."

We ate in peace for a while, just enjoying the atmosphere and the food. "When do you have to be back?" I asked the question as I tucked my cleaned plate to the side and watched her trying to tackle the rest of her burger without getting too messy.

She flipped her cell phone over and glanced down at the time. "I should be getting back soon, actually. Beth isn't stringent on my lunch break being just an hour, but I don't like to take advantage," she insisted.

"I know you don't, beautiful. Finish up and I'll walk you back before I have to head in to work for a little bit."

"Will you be coming back home tonight?" I'm not going to lie and say it didn't feel good to hear that question from her lips. She called our house her home now, and she wanted to know if I would be there with her. My heart ticked up a couple beats per minute.

"Wild horses couldn't keep me away, Anna."

Chapter 14

Evan picked me up from work the day after our lunch at the

Crab House in order to take me to my make-up doctor appointment. We were both sitting in the lobby together, waiting to be called back when I noticed a little boy who couldn't have been more than two years old. He seemed infatuated with Evan and his mom was a bit preoccupied with an infant in a car carrier. I wondered how she managed with two little ones so close in age. That had to be exhausting.

"Dada?" The little boy questioned as he moved closer with a

bit of apprehension. At first Evan didn't seem to notice, but then the little boy tugged on his jeans near his knee. "Dada?" He questioned again.

"Sorry, buddy, I'm not your guy," Evan managed to get out while trying to hide his amusement from the boy.

"Dada!" The boy demanded a bit more forcefully, not accepting Evan's answer. This caused the child's mother to finally look up. Her reddened cheeks were proof that she was embarrassed.

"Sorry," she stated quickly as she moved the couple steps away from the baby carrier that had been sitting on the floor in front of her chair in order to grab hold of her toddling son. "His dad is on deployment right now and every man he sees is suddenly Dada."

"It's okay, I've seen that happen a lot in the service," Evan answered her politely, trying to put the woman at ease with the situation.

"Well, thank God you took it okay. I've had men that heard him do that and weren't so nice. Granted, sometimes it was because the women with them were none too happy about it," she offered with a chuckle. "I swear, I'll be lucky if my son doesn't accidentally get me shot by someone's jealous woman."

My name was called as she said this, having us both stand while chuckling at her fear. "Good luck with that one," I told her as Evan grinned and waved goodbye to the little boy. "Later, little man."

"That was kind of sad," I finally managed to say after we had been moved to the back where the nurse was taking my vitals.

"That's military life for you. I really meant what I said. It's something we see all too often coming back from deployment. Young children are confused about who their returning parent is. Lots of families end up in counseling as a result, because it's tough on the kids suddenly having another parent that's been away long enough for them to forget. It's also hell on the parent who had to be away to come home only to have been forgotten. Then there's the one who has been doing it all on their own and they have to adjust to another person suddenly butting in and judging how they do things. I'm thankful my time is completely up. I never wanted to start a family while I could still be called up to duty. I don't want my kid calling every strange man he meets daddy.

Someone rapped on the door a couple times before it opened and a man poked his head around the corner. "Are you guys ready for me?" He asked, as he just continued on into the room anyway, shutting the door behind himself and his assistant. I wasn't sure if she was a nurse, an ultrasound tech, or what at that point.

"We're ready," I told him without missing a beat. "I don't want to know the sex"

"Are you sure?" The doctor asked.

"Positive. I want to be surprised."

"What about you?" The doctor asked Evan.

"I don't mind knowing, but will go along with whatever Anna decides," Evan told the man.

"Ah, smart man. Happy wife, happy life," he commented as he winked at me. I giggled before glancing over at Evan and seeing this look in his eyes that I couldn't quite understand. It wasn't nearly the molten look he had whenever he was horny. It was something warmer and deeper. It was also the first time I think he had heard someone call me his wife when we were both together, or maybe at all. The fact that it obviously affected him made me flush with warmth. The look, the feel of him in that moment, had been what was holding me back. More to the point the lack of it backing the words he was telling me had been holding me back. I simply hadn't believed he felt for me what he claimed to. I turned my attention back to what was going on around me. There was plenty of time to focus on our roller coaster ride of a relationship later.

I had been through an ultrasound before, although it wasn't going to be like the last one where my baby had been a tiny little blip on the screen that didn't really resemble more than a shrimp or something non-human. This time, I was going to see my baby looking like a baby and the excitement had me wanting to pee my pants. No, seriously. In the most literal way. "I think I might have to go to the bathroom before," I started to say, causing the doctor to chuckle.

"It might be a little uncomfortable, but honestly, it will probably help with the visuals if you can hang in there until we're done."

"Okay, well, at least I warned you, just in case," I told him. Both men were chuckling after that as the doctor squirted the pre-warmed gel onto my belly. Once he put the wand over my belly he flicked something on the machine and the baby's heartbeat came through loud and clear. I glanced over at Evan knowing he didn't understand what he was hearing. "That's the baby's heartbeat," I explained.

"Why is it so fast?"

"Not to worry, that's a healthy rate at this stage in the game," my doctor informed him. We watched as he took some measurements, and then he pointed out the beating heart to Evan as well as the fact that our little one was sucking it's thumb. I didn't know where to focus my attention. The screen with my baby was beyond fascinating, but Evan's face was almost as priceless. I could see the sheen of moisture in his eyes as he watched everything with hawk-like attentiveness. Then I saw the moment realization dawned in his eyes and he grinned. The doctor had a similar expression as if they'd just shared a silent secret, and when I glanced over toward the monitor the doctor quickly jerked his hand across my belly looking for a different angle. They weren't fooling anyone. He'd just seen the sex of the baby. I couldn't even be mad at him because he didn't say a word about it. He just kept smiling through the rest of the appointment.

"As you know, the results of the amnio came back before with everything looking good. There didn't seem to be anything in the results we need to worry about. Your sugar test last time also came back within acceptable parameters. Keep eating healthy and getting plenty of exercise. You're doing well, and the baby is measuring right on track with your due date." I figured he was reiterating things for Evan since he hadn't been with me at the last appointment. My doctor wasn't stupid. He knew we had a DNA test done then. So, it made sense in most cases that this would be the appointment where the person proven to be the dad might show up.

"Do either of you have any questions for me?"

Neither of us spoke. Evan's eyes were still glued to the screen before the doctor removed the wand and started wiping the gel off it and then off of my belly. "You can grab one of our cards on the way out and if you think of something later, feel free to call. Any of the nurses should be able to answer most of what you might have to ask." He then printed off a few things and pulled a flash drive from the machine before handing it over to Evan.

"What's this?"

"I thought you might want pictures to remember today by."

Evan glanced down at the printed black and white pictures as well. "Thank you," Evan stated clearly, but I could hear the gravely layer to his voice that made it impossible for him to hide the emotion he was feeling.

It didn't take long to get cleaned up, schedule my next appointment, and then get out to where the truck was parked. Once Evan made sure I was inside and buckled in, he climbed in the driver's side and took another look at the images he'd been handed. That was when he fell apart.

"Evan?" I asked as he leaned his head against the steering wheel while holding the images out to his side so I could take them. "Are you okay?" I asked when he didn't answer.

"Just, need a minute." We sat in the quiet of the truck cab as I watched his shoulders shake a bit before he finally got himself together and glanced red-rimmed eyes over at me. "I almost missed all of this," he whispered as his balled fist rubbed across his chest where his heart was, as if to alleviate an ache there. "I'm so sorry for everything, Anna. I don't know how to make you believe that, but I will never stop trying to prove to you how sorry I am and how none of it will ever happen again."

I took my phone out of my purse and texted Beth before I could respond to him.

Me: I'm not going to make it back today.

Beth: It's okay, slow here. Think I'm going to just close up shop early and get some shopping done. Everything okay?

Me: It's fine. Evan needs me though. It was very emotional.

Beth: Enjoy the rest of your day, honey.

"How about you take me home and I'll make us an early dinner?" I suggested after I had the go-ahead to take the rest of the day off guilt free.

"What about work?"

"I just checked with Beth. It's fine. Let's go home."

I thought I heard him repeat the word home, but it was said so low, I couldn't be sure. Before I could question it, he had the truck started and about to back out of the parking spot before he stopped and threw the truck back in park. "I need to get this off my chest now," he told me when I turned to ask why he had changed his mind.

"That was our baby. We saw our baby today sucking on its thumb in your belly."

"We did," I agreed.

"I never want to miss out on another thing, Anna. Please, promise me that I won't have to."

I scooted over on the bench seat so that our sides were touching and I reached up to cup his jaw in my hand feeling the course hairs of the short beard he had started to grow tickle my palm. "I promise you." My words were softly spoken, but I don't think they made near the impact as the gesture that followed them. I leaned in and placed my lips to his, sealing that promise with a kiss. His gasped intake of air showed just how surprised he was that I had done it. That only lasted a moment before he pulled me closer still, locking one hand around my neck with the other on my thigh as he deepened the kiss. Good gravy, that kiss would have knocked me flat on my butt had I not already been sitting.

It took me a couple minutes to come back to reality and attempt to peel myself out of Evan's grasp. When I did, I glanced away quickly, embarrassed that I allowed the simple gesture of a kiss to go too far. The moment I glanced away, my world fell to pieces, I started hyperventilating, and all I could do was point a finger in the direction of pure evil. "That's…" I didn't even finish my sentence when I saw the woman duck into a store across the street. No way was I letting her get out of my sight. I jumped from the truck and took off across the road. Evan caught up to me quickly and snagged my arm just before I made it inside the store.

"What the hell is going on?"

"I just saw Seneca," I whispered. "She just went inside the store."

"Are you sure? She's supposed to be in jail, Anna. She couldn't be out here. The club would have heard about her getting out.

"Of course I'm sure. I'll never forget her face as long as I live. She took my brother from us."

I watched as Evan took out his phone and dialed. He held

me close to his body as we stood there basically guarding the front doors from anyone who might come out of them.

"We have a problem," he said immediately when someone picked up. "Seneca is out. She's in a store downtown right now." Evan stopped and listened before glancing down at me again. Then he answered whatever question I couldn't hear from the other end. "Anna spotted her. Pretty sure. She's shaken up. I had to stop her from chasing after the bitch."

He listened a few more minutes and then hung up. "Kane is on his way since he's closest. I want you to go wait in the truck with the doors locked baby. We already know what this whore is capable of. I refuse to risk you or the baby. No arguments."

Kane pulled up just as I was locking myself in the truck. He spoke to Kane, and then we watched as Kane moved to go inside the store. Not a minute later J-Bird rolled up and wasn't even off his bike yet before screaming at Evan.

"What the fuck are you doing standing around out here, Joker?"

"I had to stay with Anna, asshole. Kane's inside. Go help him."

J-Bird barely made it to the door before Kane was manhandling the woman out the front door. They brought her over to the truck and glanced at their two bikes. "There's no way either of us can ride with her on our bikes. She's capable of anything."

"I'm not getting on a motorcycle with either of you crazy idiots. Let me go. I'll scream for the police."

"Good then they can lock you up since you're supposed to be in jail anyway."

"No, I'm…" the woman got no more out before J-Bird pinched down on a pressure point near her neck, shutting her up.

"We need your truck," he stated in his no-nonsense way he had adapted since everything that had happened with Ever and the tattoos she had put on the men of the club.

"I get that, but I can't put Anna on a bike either," Evan argued.

"Joker," Kane called out. "Ever is on her way to get Anna. You can ride my bike back to the clubhouse when she gets here. I'll go in the truck with J-Bird. She ain't gonna stay out much longer." He tipped his head down to indicate the woman who was starting to stir a bit. They quickly shifted so that I was out of the truck, J-Bird was in the driver's seat and Kane was securing the woman in the passenger seat. Then they were gone while Evan stood waiting with me for Ever who showed up about three minutes later.

"How is she free right now?" I asked as Ever pulled up in front of us.

"I don't know, beautiful. That's what we're going to find out. Stay with Ever."

"Heck no. That woman killed our brother. If you think you could keep either of us away you are dead wrong."

"Fine. Follow me there," he told Ever as I got inside her car.

"What's going on?"

"We just saw Seneca out on the street. She went into the shop over there. They guys came and dragged her out and just took off with her to the clubhouse," I explained to my sister.

"What the absolute fuck?"

"Let's go find out," I told her impatiently.

Chapter 15

RATTLED

I rolled up the clubhouse with Ever hot on my wheels. Once the girls were out of the car and we managed to get into the clubhouse, I maneuvered them over to the bar. "I want the two of you to take a seat, and wait here while we figure this out. I know Toby was your brother, but you need to let the brothers do what they do. I'll come let you know as much as I can in just a bit." I leaned in and kissed the top of Anna's head, ready to leave when her hand snaked out and caught a hold of mine to stop me.

"I need to call Gretchen." It was a demand, but considering she was telling me she was doing it, she was also asking permission in a way, which I respected.

"No. You know how club business works, Anna. She's never officially been a part of the club since Toby didn't claim her."

"That woman you guys have here murdered her man and her baby. It's her business more than any of yours!" She shouted the words out, bringing all the activity in the room to halt.

Double-D had come through the doors just in time to hear her. "Let us find out what's going on before we go upsetting Gretchen, okay? No point telling her we have that bitch here when we don't have answers ourselves yet. Can you just wait until we know what's going on?"

"Fine," Anna huffed as Lucy and Tiger Lily came barreling through the door and headed straight for Anna and Ever.

Double-D and I made our way down to the interrogation room the club had made out of an old, defunct swimming pool that had been covered over years ago. The deepest end was left for any wet work that the club might need done. The shallow end had been dug out more to accommodate the height of a bunch of bikers who got really tired of bending over practically in half when they needed use of the place. There was a smaller tunnel extending off the back that led to hidden stairs under a shed on the property, which was how we entered the space. The minute we had made our way down the stairs we could hear the yelling.

"You killed my best fucking friend, my brother! You think you can just go waltzing around our town free as you please?" J-Bird's words were spat out at the woman with enough venom that words alone should have been her end. Merc nodded to us, appearing thankful for our arrival. Deck was already there trying to pull J-Bird, and the knife he wielded, away from the frightened woman.

"I t-t-told you," she insisted even with the slight stutter that was no doubt brought on by her sheer terror. "My name is Clem. Seneca is my sister. My twin. She is still in jail. That's why I came here to tell her goodbye once and for all. This was the last straw with our family. My parents refused to come." She babbled the words out and while every person in the room could taste the fear in every single one spoken, she did not cry or blubber as she spoke. "You can check. It's not like the jail could keep it a secret if my evil twin managed to spring herself from their clutches."

"Kane!" Merc called out. "Head on over to the jail. Do not leave until you can get eyes on Seneca and let us know." Kane didn't even respond. He simply turned and left the underground facility. It was somewhat damp down here as Charleston wasn't exactly the best place to have an underground anything. The city was less than 20 feet above sea level and the humidity in the area far too high.

"I need your full name, darlin'." Merc was putting on the friendly, charming persona he often used with women that had them eating out of his hand when necessary. The woman sighed, her shoulders drooping as she did. She must have felt like someone finally believed her.

"You can check my wallet in my back pocket," she stated as she stood from the chair she'd been seated in. Her hands were tied in front of her with a zip tie so she cocked her hip to the side to show that the wallet she spoke of was in her back pocket. J-Bird didn't hesitate and moved in to snatch the wallet out. It was a worn down leather wallet with a snap closure, one a man would normally use. J-Bird, shirking protocol, opened the thing up and rifled through it until he found the woman's driver's license.

"Clemson Holly Davis," he read off the license and then gave the woman an odd look. "Who the fuck names their daughter Clemson?"

"A mother who named the first born twin after the town we were made in and the second after the place we were born," she answered snidely as she plopped back down in the chair. Clearly, she knew leaving wasn't going to be an option until we had eyes on her sister. "Listen, I get it. I won't tell anyone about what happened here today. I'd have probably done the same damn thing if I were you and saw me wandering around town." She shook her head and then let it hang loosely there on her shoulders. "I still can't believe she did what they've accused her of. I don't doubt she's capable, but I never thought she'd…" The woman glanced up, avoiding J-Bird, and set her eyes on Double-D and myself. "I'm so sorry for the loss of your man."

"My son," Double-D corrected and was rewarded for the two words by the woman's wince. "Their club brother, best friend, nephew," he pointed in turn at J-Bird and Merc. "My girls are upstairs waiting to know why the cunt who killed their brother is walking free. His woman, who lost their baby during Seneca Davis's rampage, will also want to know."

The girl furrowed her brow. "His woman? He had a woman who was pregnant? I thought my sister was dating the man. She told us she saw him with another woman, and lost it."

"Your sister," he spat the words, showing he wasn't so certain he believed her story yet despite the state issued identification with a different name. She was a club whore, available to any of the men for them to use for sex. My son said he only went there once and she had been following him around for months afterward. We caught her creeping around outside of our own home just a couple days prior to her taking my son from us."

"Oh God," the woman panted out. She was just now starting to see the trouble she might be in. Even if she turned out to be who she claimed to be, we were the big bad bikers who had her held captive in an underground facility. We were also the bikers

235

who were probably looking for retribution for what her sister had taken from us. "I always knew that bitch would get me killed," she muttered. No one spoke after that. We watched as J-Bird paced the floor. Merc just stood with his back to one of the walls and watched his son's movements. Double-D never took his eyes off the woman seated before us, and I was watchful of all of them. We waited an hour for Kane to return.

He didn't say a word as he moved directly to Merc and handed him a cell phone. Merc took it and tapped and scrolled on the screen. "Thanks," he told Kane as he handed the phone back and nodded to Double-D who was next to go through whatever Kane was showing them. J-Bird's curiosity got the better of him and he went to look to.

"Fuck!" He hissed out before glancing back over his shoulder toward the woman. "We can't just let her go now."

"We can, and we will. She's not going to say a word because she understands why and what we thought," Merc stated coolly as he glared at her.

"I do understand. You don't have to worry about that."

"We're not in the habit of killing women," he went on, seemingly ignoring her words. "Make no mistake, if we find out you spoke one fucking word about what happened here today, to anyone, I will rescind that rule and we will bury you beside your sister."

"She's in jail, not dead," Clem announced.

"For now," J-Bird finished and eyed the woman with meaning.

"I see." She paled, but managed to keep herself together. "I just came to town to watch the trial and say goodbye. It didn't sit right with me that she had killed her man in a fit of a jealousy. She doesn't get jealous. I don't think my sister has any real emotions anymore," the woman spilled her family's secrets.

"She tried to kill herself twice now," I put in. "Someone who is suicidal usually has some emotions."

Clem laughed. "You would think, but I guarantee her little attempts were very calculated. She was buying time. A trial should have already happened by now. It's been the better part of a year. Do not doubt for a minute that my sister has some devious plan cooked up. She's been a little off our whole lives, but it got a lot worse during our teen years." She shook her head again as if willing the memories away. "You know how people joke about having an evil twin out there somewhere? I grew up with everyone who knew us understanding just how true that statement could be. This isn't the first time I suffered because I look like her either," she proclaimed and we could all see how she visibly shuddered. "At least you guys actually checked to make sure you had the right person before it got…" she breathed out and then added one more word. "Personal."

Damn, but I was curious about her story. I didn't think it was something we were going to end up privy to though. "Jay, give

237

the lady a ride back to where you found her," Merc ordered before turning back to the woman in question. "One word is all it will take and this won't have a happy ending for you. I'm sorry your sister got you into this mess, but keeping that in mind, maybe once you see her you need to be on your way out of town."

She nodded and stood to follow J-Bird out of the building. He stopped her before they got to the end of the tunnel and placed something around her head so she couldn't see where she was coming from when they left. Once they were topside, Kane spoke up. "I need to go let Gretchen know in case she accidentally runs into her. The woman wasn't too far from her sister's photography studio when we grabbed her.

"Do us a favor, and just go pick her up and bring her here, yeah?" Double-D asked. At first it seemed as though Kane would deny the request, but thinking better of it, he nodded his head before he left to go do just that.

"You think it's wise bringing her in on this?" Merc asked my father-in-law.

"Toby would want us to make sure she knows and that she's protected. We don't know how tight those sisters actually are. Her good twin bullshit could have just been an act. Until we know for sure, I'd like to keep a man on her."

"Kane seems to be the best for the job since he's a prospect and works with her over at Permanent Marks," Merc suggested.

"He also seems a little too interested in her," Double-D spat out while eyeing the tunnel Kane had gone down only moments ago.

"He's been gone a while now. She can't grieve forever, D. You're going to have to be okay with seeing her move on, even if it is with a brother."

"Fuck!" Double-D yelled as he lashed out and kicked the chair that Clem had been sitting in so hard it broke into pieces on impact with the concrete wall. "I want eyes on the twin until we know for sure she's out of town," Double-D ordered, not giving one fuck that he wasn't Prez here. We all knew he was lashing out because this was bringing on a world of pain where his dead son, grandbaby, and the woman they left behind were concerned. I finally understood why Kane had asked the questions he did when we were on our run to Jacksonville though. It wasn't Ever he was interested in at all. It had been Gretchen this whole time.

"Already handled," Merc explained as he tucked his cell back into the front pocket of his jeans.

Chapter 16

SETTLED

It took two months for the dust to settle after the Davis twin

had been discovered. She stuck around town for a little more
than a week, but after realizing she would have a crazed J-Bird
following her everywhere, she finally left town. After all the
initial delays due to her multiple suicide attempts and her lawyers
delaying for various reasons, Seneca's trial was finally able to
move forward, despite the fact that her attorneys tried to
forestall the proceedings again one final time, stating that their

client was not of sound mind to stand trial. The claim was that she suffered multiple personality disorder, and believed that she was her twin sister locked up unfairly. No doubt, she had gotten the idea when her sister visited. It didn't work though. The trial went on, and within a month, she was convicted and sentenced to thirty years in prison with no option for parole.

Thirty years didn't seem like a long enough time considering all the years we would now lose out on with my brother and the entire lifetime his baby lost out on. Somehow though, I didn't think the club would allow her to serve out those thirty years in peace, so that was at least something.

Watching the trial commence and having to testify about Seneca stalking Toby as well as the day everything happened, took a toll on Gretchen. The bit of healing she had done slipped away and she was back to her sullen grief-filled existence. Ever and I worked with Beth to make sure she was never alone for too long, but with me moving further along in my pregnancy, it was becoming difficult to hold up my end so Kane and Zeke started taking turns too.

Evan and I also had a chance to grow closer over the last two months of living in the same house. We weren't lovers again by any stretch of the imagination. He hadn't even kissed me again since that one moment just after the ultrasound. I was so torn about everything going on between us. I wanted him to kiss me. I actually needed him to kiss me again, and I wasn't really sure what was holding him back at this point. I had forgiven him. I was pretty sure I had. Now, I had started to worry that maybe he just wasn't attracted to me anymore. I was seven months along in my pregnancy, and my body had changed so much. I had a nearly D-cup breast for the first time in my life, my butt could be the envy of any Kardashian fan. Those were the good attributes in a man's eyes, I supposed. Then again, there was the giant belly with the stretch marks, and the weird brown line that ran from my belly button to my pubic region. I wasn't exactly sure if it went all the way to my girl parts because I could no longer see past my belly to shave very well down there. I managed to keep the sides trimmed up, but straight beneath my belly was a lost world to me now.

Maybe he had seen at some point and was turned off by the fact that my lady garden now looked like an overrun forest? I didn't know, but that was possible. I missed being intimate with Evan. For the past two months, instead of waking to dreams of us together before, I woke to dreams of that day outside of the doctor's office. In some of my dreams, I never saw Seneca's twin sister and we went straight home and made love together. I woke up just two mornings ago having had such a vivid version of that dream that I actually woke to myself climaxing. My body was feverish, I was so wet between my legs, I worried momentarily that my water had broken, and my poor belly was having weird contractions going hard as stone and then softening up. The pleasure piercing through my nerve endings was the thing that tipped me off as to what happened. I didn't even know it was possible to have an orgasm without touching yourself.

Still, Evan wouldn't touch me anymore beyond a hug or hand holding, so I was left with the worries that started to flood my brain whenever he was gone from the house. If he wasn't attracted to me anymore, would he stray? Would he find someone he was attracted to? I was in the midst of wandering thoughts just like those when the door opened at just before 11 pm. Our normal routine had been that if I was awake when he came home, he would immediately come to me and touch my belly and talk to our baby. As he moved closer to do just that I smelled it. A cloying sweetness clung to him and turned my stomach with each step that drew him closer and made the smell more prominent.

I sidestepped him when he got close enough to attempt to reach out for my belly. "You smell like skank," I informed him.

He laughed at my response as I stood there glaring at him. He soon realized he better start explaining why he smelled like skank. "I was at the club with Deck to see Double-D."

"So you got a lap dance or a private room show?" I asked accusingly.

"Neither. Two of the fucking dancers broke out in a biting, nail-scratching, hair-pulling brawl. Deck grabbed one and I took the other and pulled her off to the side for the staff to deal with.

Your dad and Deck were there the whole time, beautiful. They can tell you. Now, get over here and let me have my baby belly time," he demanded.

I shook my head back and forth. "Nope. Go shower first. You stink," I told him as I wrinkled my nose and started rubbing my temples with my fingers. The smell really was incredibly strong.

His face dropped, but he turned and moved to do as I had asked while I plopped my big butt down on the sofa to wait. My whole body was vibrating with pent up emotion. I couldn't stop those images I'd conjured just moments before he came through the door from filtering in as the scent of stripper floated in the air. Those same worries and insecurities came flooding back to me. With a strange woman's scent in the air – even though I had been given a reason for it – my brain decided that my fears were true. It might not have happened tonight, but Evan had already proven that the only interest he still had in my body – even after seeing a stripper throw down – was to say hello to my baby bump.

When she told me to go get a shower before touching her, I

knew there was more to the request than the nasty, sickly-sweet perfume left clinging to my clothing from the bitch I had pulled off of Roxy – the newest star of the recently opened strip club. It was modeled after a club we had in South Dakota called Renegade Rosy's, and seemed to already be drawing a larger crowd than the others.

I stood under the hot water of the shower, scrubbing vigorously at my skin to free it of that scent when I laughed at the fact that the smell wasn't the only thing I had to get rid of. There was glitter falling down, probably from my hair or neck somewhere, that must have been transferred from the stripper I'd picked up. That shit was like a disease you couldn't get rid of. For every shiny fleck I washed away, there seemed to be two more bright and shiny spots that would spawn in its place.

It wasn't until I finished up in the shower and made my way back to the living room that my suspicions had been confirmed. Anna was sitting there on the couch staring off into space, not even realizing I was back in the room and there were fresh tears tracking down her face. I suddenly felt like the world's biggest asshole. I should have showered at the clubhouse so that I didn't come home looking or smelling like that. More importantly though, I knew this was about our wedding night all over again. She tried to tell herself that she had forgiven me for that, but it was obvious that even if she had forgiven, she would never forget. Deck's words from that day when I woke up with the wrong woman in my arms came back to haunt me.

"This shit you pulled on that girl's wedding night? She will never be able to forget this." His words rang truer in my head now than they had at the time. It had been so many months, and still my actions hung between us and weighed her down. I turned my focus back toward Anna instead of memories of the past too. No use in us both getting lost there.

"It's okay, you know?" Anna finally said, making me realize she had, in fact, realized I was there.

"What's okay?"

"That you're with other women instead of me. I understand you're not attracted to me like that anymore. It just took me a while to get it."

"To get what exactly?" I clipped out, getting angrier at the situation with every word she spoke.

"We've been working on a friendship this whole time. I thought it might have been more, but I get it now."

"No! Clearly, you don't get it – at all!"

"But…"

"But what?"

"We don't have sex," she admitted.

"No, we don't. This is why we don't." I explained my way of thinking to her, or thought that was enough for her to get my meaning. I realized it wasn't when she just stared at me with a confused look on her face. "When you tried to come on to me, or touch me, before what did I tell you each time?"

"That the time wasn't right," she stated grudgingly.

"Anna we're still building trust here along with our friendship. I haven't been with anyone else. I don't want anyone else. I'm fucking desperate to get my hands on you again and seeing you growing rounder with our child isn't helping matters any. You're beyond fucking gorgeous. But we're not there yet, as much as it pains me to admit that. This conversation proves that. How long have you been wondering if I was sleeping around on you?" She didn't answer, but the guilty expression she wore spoke volumes. "The fact that you couldn't just ask me tells me I was right to wait. Anna, I fucked up enough already where you're concerned. I won't do it again."

"I'm sorry," she whispered through her tears.

"Don't be sorry, beautiful. This was my own doing. Just know that it's only you. Well, thoughts of you and my hand, until you're ready. Until we're both ready, okay?"

"Okay," she agreed softly.

"I love you, Anna."

"I never stopped loving you," she admitted. "Even when you were a horrible person who I disliked immensely; I never could tell my heart to stop beating for you."

"Shit! You're killing me, here, beautiful."

"I hope not," she teased while trying to dry her eyes with the neckline of her oversized t-shirt. "This baby needs a daddy."

"I know it. Now, bring my belly to me," I commanded while thrusting my grabby hands out to her, making her giggle. "That's my girl." I praised her before turning my attention to the other most important person in my life. "Daddy loves you, baby."

Chapter 17

PICTURE PERFECT

I handed our last customer her package of photos before she

walked out the door, all smiles. It actually lifted my spirits to work here for that reason. Making people happy was a joy of mine, and seeing them leave the studio with looking pleased as punch always brightened my days. Not that my days weren't already bright. Evan and I had spent the past week watching movies, cooking together, and simply existing in one another's space with no pressure or expectations and it had been divine.

I'd also supervised when he started putting together the crib, changing table, and had a glider rocker put in the spare room. The bed in there was now pushed as far up against the wall, beside the door to get into the room, as it could go.

Evan talked about just putting a twin size bed in there and taking the full-size one out so there was more room, but I didn't think he'd fit well enough on a twin considering his size. I had nearly invited him to just come sleep in the master bedroom's king-size be with me, but I didn't think I could handle the rejection if he told me no. I knew his reasoning, but my heart wouldn't hear reason. It would simply hear the no, so I had kept my mouth shut. The tinkling of the bell as my customer made her way out the door and to her car pulled me back to the task at hand. I started going through appointments to see what we would have to handle tomorrow and, just as I was about to let Beth know we didn't have anything on the books until after noon tomorrow, a white-hot pain shot through my back and wrapped around my hips, before dipping low into my belly as if I'd been whipped from the inside out and back to front.

"Ouch," I murmured as I leaned forward on the counter and tried to catch my breath. I had just managed to get myself under control when Beth stuck her head out of the back room where she took a lot of her in-studio photos.

"We don't have anyone else in the book for today, do we?" She asked.

"No, we don't and Candace just left. She was thrilled with her photos."

"Good! I'm so happy to hear that. I don't suppose you'd like to come back and sit for some pregnancy photos, would you?"

"Really?" Excitement coursed through me at the prospect. I don't know why I hadn't thought of doing any maternity photos before, especially considering where I worked, but now I wanted to jump for joy at the prospect. "I'd love to!"

"Great! Flip the sign to closed, lock the door, and waddle your butt back here then."

"I'm not a penguin!" I shouted at her as I turned the sign and locked the front door.

"Could have fooled me," she shouted.

I did exactly as she asked and waddled my ever-growing behind into the back studio space where she already had a pretty little garden scene drawn down. I stood in front of it and allowed her to position me just so before she moved back behind her camera. "Say fuzzy pickles!"

I scrunched my nose up at the thought of fuzzy pickles just as Beth clicked. She giggled. "Okay, well that one works with the kids. I'll have to remember the adult reaction is to be grossed out."

"Where in the world did you even come up with that?" Beth just shrugged. "And what in the world is a fuzzy pickle? I just thought about a moldy dog turd and now I'm kind of glad I

251

haven't felt like eating lunch yet."

Beth laughed as she changed some setting or other on her camera. I doubled over a little, again feeling that pain wrap around my mid-section from back to front. Beth thought I was just pretending to be sick. I didn't correct her, though I was beginning to worry a bit. Something didn't feel right.

"Okay, here's a stool, I want you to just sit on it and frame your hands on your belly like this," Beth moved my hands so that my fingers were forming a little heart over my belly.

"Aw, that's sweet," I told her as I also noticed the heart background she had queued up for this shot.

"Isn't it?" She snapped a couple shots and then asked me to stand.

"Okay for this one, I want to get a picture of you facing out into the next scene and…"

"You're taking a picture of my giant rear end?" I asked aghast at my friend and employer for suggesting such a thing.

"It'll probably get cropped from the waist up with you looking back at me over your shoulder," she suggested. "It's just something I've been wanting to test out."

"Fine, but if I see you using my butt as target practice in here one day I'm not going to be happy." Beth laughed at that because before I started working here, she and Gretchen used to print out a picture of their worst clients and use them for target practice on a dart board.

"Okay, stand just like that while I raise the heart backdrop. The one I want to use is underneath of it," Beth was saying as she clicked a button and the motor started whirring as the backdrop began to roll back up. Beth had moved to a camera that was located off to the side of me, which was weird.

"I thought you were testing a shot from the back, there's no…" I stopped mid-sentence as a pair of jeans came into view, along with a singular motorcycle boot. Singular because these particular denim-clad legs were on bended knee in front of me. "Oh my word," I whispered through my hands that had automatically gone to my face to hide my surprise. As the backdrop continued up, the rest of Evan came into view. He was grinning up at me from where he had bent a knee and held a small, white jewelry box out. His hazel-green eyes glittered like jewels in the lighting Beth had set up, and his smile both asked the question for him and left him looking sheepish all at once. He wasn't sure how I would react to what he was doing, that was for sure.

"What are you doing?" I asked stupidly.

"Asking you to marry me." His answer was so simple, and yet it was wildly unexpected.

"We're already married."

"Nah, we signed a contract. Right now, I'm trying to put a ring on your finger, and asking you to be mine forever because I'm so in love with you, beautiful. I don't want to spend another day without you. You may already be my wife legally, but I want you to be my wife in all the other ways too."

"Evan," I managed to puff out on another whisper. There was no way this whole scene was real. I was about to ask if he was serious when another pain ripped through my abdomen and had me bending in two to catch my breath. I barely managed to bite back the yelp of pain that threatened to let loose, but the whimper that came after made its way out to the ears of the people in the room anyway.

"Anna, are you okay?" He started to get to his feet, but I put out my arm to touch his shoulders and hold him in place. "I'm fine. I don't think a ring will fit on my puffy fingers right now though."

"Is that a yes?" He asked while grinning up at me.

"Yes, Evan."

He jumped up and pulled me into his body, placing a sweet kiss on my lips as he moved my hair out of the way and clasped a necklace around my neck. I glanced down to see a gorgeous ring attached to the white gold chain. "Once you've gone through all the post-partum stuff we'll have it sized for you," he told me as his hands slid from my neck to my shoulders, and down my arms before they found a resting place on my belly. Then he got down on his knees once more and proudly told my belly, "She said yes!"

He received a swift kick as his response, just before the

white-hot pain ripped through my body again.

"Anna!" He yelled. Then he was barking orders to Beth as I doubled over again. Within minutes, an ambulance was taking me to the hospital. Evan was sitting to my side out of the way of the paramedic lady who was hooking my body up to a bunch of monitors.

"It's still too early," I cried.

"You will be fine," he tried to assure me.

"The baby!" I cried some more.

"Both of my girls are going to be just fine." I was going to ignore that he just let the gender slip since he was worried about us.

"Ma'am, when was the last time you felt the baby move?" That came from the paramedic woman who had been attaching everything.

"Just now. The baby just kicked me."

"That's good. Don't worry, we're going to get you taken care of," she insisted.

Two days later, I was finally being released from the hospital with orders to be on bed rest at home. The doctors had hooked me up to an IV with a drip of Magnesium to help stop the labor, and I was given a series of things to continue doing or stop doing while at home to increase the chances that I could carry the baby to a healthier date.

Evan stayed by my side the entire time I was in the hospital. He refused to leave, even when visiting hours were over. It was sweet to see how protective he was over the baby and me, especially when he practically threw one of the nurses out of the room when she couldn't get the IV started properly. After the third unsuccessful stick, he told her if she tried to get near me with anything sharp again, she'd find that IV stuck somewhere she'd have a hard time retrieving it from without surgical intervention. Needless to say, someone else had managed to get the IV started after that without any problem.

You would think that lying around in a bed for nearly 48 hours straight would mean you'd have plenty of energy when you finally managed to get up, but just the walk to the truck tuckered me out, and I ended up nodding off on the way home.

"Anna," I heard him whisper before he gently touched my arm. "We're home, beautiful."

"Okay," I managed to get out, even though my voice was slightly muffled by the sleepiness still trying to hold me under its spell. He helped me out of the truck and then stayed by my side the whole way into the house. The moment we walked through the door, I noticed what he had done. The silver of the frame glinted from the sun coming in through the door drawing my focus. There, just above the mantel, was a larger version of the picture frame I'd purchased all those years ago to use for my wedding photos. Instead of it only holding two 5x7 images, this one held two 8x10 images and in the middle there was an engraving inside a silver heart that simply stated, Family First, Love Always.

The picture to the left of the engraving was a picture of Evan proposing to me. Beth must have been clicking away during the whole surprise engagement. The picture to the right was of Evan on his knees in front of me when he kissed my belly and then announced to the baby, "She said yes."

I sniffled back the emotion I was feeling seeing those two pictures, knowing he understood the significance they would hold. He was trying to give me memories that I should have had from the beginning, and I loved him all the more for it.

"I think I want to stay out here on the couch instead of the bed," I told him as I continued staring at the images on our living room wall.

"As happy as I am that you enjoy my present that much, I think you better stay in the bedroom. You'll be more comfortable. I can move that into the bedroom for you, if you'd like."

"No. It stays," I pouted, and then reluctantly moved toward the bedroom leaving the images behind.

Chapter 18

TIME'S UP

JOKER

I had never been so scared as the day I proposed to Anna. I

was on edge already, worried she would say no. Sure, we were already married, but me asking her, and actually going through with it without either of us feeling forced or obligated was something I had been thinking about for a long time. There was a bit of ulterior motive too. Anna had shit memories of our first wedding, she didn't have any engagement memories. I wanted to start flooding her with the things she wanted to remember in order to help her move past the shit we both wished wasn't still in our heads sometimes when we closed our eyes at night.

Then she said yes, and I was elated until she doubled over for the second time, unable to disguise the pain she was in that time. It was too early for our daughter to be born. Not that she knew we were having a girl, but I did. It was just too damn early. Thankfully, the doctor got her labor stopped and bed rest has kept our baby inside of her these past six weeks. Though, it's probably a good thing that Anna wasn't going to be on bed rest much longer, because she was starting to get pretty fucking cranky.

"I hate this fudging bed!" She screamed from the bedroom when I opened the door to see who had been knocking.

"I'd ask how things are going, but I'm guessing it's been a lot of that," Deck laughed as he pointed toward the small hallway that led to the bedrooms.

"Yeah, so you remember when your wife wanted to take her to live with you guys a few months ago? I'm thinking you should…"

"I can hear you!" Anna called out. "You better shut your darn pie hole. You aren't the one stuck in the same room all the friggin' time."

"Your vocabulary has become worrisome, little Miss Anna," Deck teased.

"Shut the front door, Deck!"

We both turned to look at the already closed front door before realizing what she had meant. "I do not envy you. I hope Ever isn't like that when I knock her up."

"You planning on having a baby soon?" I asked, almost relieved that I'd have a friend my age going through the same shit.

"Fuck no! We're going to have some fun first. Ever's had a tough enough time over the past few years. We're trying to enjoy time together, getting her established as an artist, and all that good shit. The kids can wait until later."

The disappointment must have shown on my face because he laughed at me. The bastard stood there and laughed in my face some more because I most definitely wasn't getting any of the fun times and adjustment times he spoke of. I was growing bored with my own hand, and that was when Anna's jerkoff radar didn't have her yelling out demands for more shit she wasn't able to get up and fetch for herself. Even her own mom – the saint that Lucy was – took a break to get away from her demanding daughter. We couldn't even watch movies together or play games because she either got too emotional or ended up falling asleep on me.

"You wouldn't change a thing," Deck announced after watching my thoughts play out on my features. I just shook my head.

"No, I wouldn't. Have you seen her? She has this cute

beachball belly going on, and she's always glowing even when she's being demanding as shit."

"Jesus, you're fucked."

"In the best way," I admitted as we moved back to the room so I could bring Anna the water she had requested before I heard the knock on the door.

"Hey, Anna Banana!" Deck teased her as he entered the room. "How are you feeling today?"

"I'm…"Anna stopped speaking so abruptly my full attention turned back to her. "Um, not so good, actually. I think I just peed."

"You just what?" I pulled the cover down off of her legs and sure enough there was a huge wet spot on her nightgown and soaking through the sheets around her. Thank fuck I had listened to her nurse at the last check up and put a mattress protector on the bed. Anna winced, drawing my attention back up to her face and then I glanced at the cute little beach ball belly I'd been talking about. It looked tight as fuck.

"Anna," I huffed out. "I don't think you peed. I'm pretty sure your water broke."

"I'll call everyone," Deck managed to say before he backed out of the room looking almost as white as the sheets did before my wife wet them.

"I have your bag, babe. You think you can walk?"

"I can do it," she insisted.

"Okay, but if you can't, Deck can grab the bag and I can carry you."

"You can't carry me!" Her voice was a shrill, squeaky thing. "I look like a whole herd of buffalo right now. You'll break your back and we'll both be broken and in bed." She sighed and the tears fell. "Then our baby won't love us because we'll be puddles of goo on the sheets."

"What?" I asked as I stared in horror at the woman I love. She just nodded her head as if I had been agreeing with her. "It's true," she said before she had to stop shuffling along because a contraction hit her with force this time. She was trying to be a champ and breathe through it, while I was ready to punch something for making my woman hurt. Myself. I would have to punch myself for this since I was the one who knocked her up in the first place.

"I'm so sorry beautiful," I told her.

"Well, you should be. Our child doesn't want a herd of buffalo for a mom."

"Do women actually go crazy during labor?" I asked Deck from over my shoulder.

"How the fuck should I know that?"

"I don't know. Call Lucy and ask her. Tell her I need her to meet us at the hospital quick-like."

"They're already on the way. At the rate we're going, they'll probably beat us there and we'll be rolling in with a kid we delivered on the front stoop," he rushed out in an exasperated tone. Then, before either of us could stop him, Deck reached down and picked Anna up. He carried her all the way to the truck. "Sorry, Anna Banana. I don't plan on playing catcher for my niece or nephew today though. Let's make the doctor work for his paycheck, yeah?"

I couldn't argue with that and managed to get us to the hospital in under fifteen minutes. Anna still had three weeks until her due date, but we were still well within the range where a healthy delivery wasn't out of the question.

"Has her water broken?" A nurse was asking as she was getting us checked in. We had already pre-registered after Anna had been admitted the first time when premature labor started.

"Either that or she pissed the bed like a toddler," I told her.

"Joker!" Anna yelped. I knew she was pissed about it since she failed to use my given name and instead used my road name. I just grinned down at her.

"It's okay, beautiful. I'll get you some depends and baby wipes from the gift shop."

"Son of a biscuit! I'm going to shave your genitals and glue it to your face. Ball hair eyebrows. I'm going to use Gorilla Glue so that crap really sticks too."

The nurse chuckled at Anna's creative threats. "Don't worry, honey. I'll help you out. Sister solidarity!" She was cheering my woman's nutso behavior on like it was the norm. Who knew,

263

maybe it was. I gave the nurse a weary look and took a step back, covering my sensitive areas as I did. I noticed Deck did the same. Neither of us were feeling too secure any longer.

"Sugar Honey Iced Tea!" My woman yelled out as she clutched her belly. "Oh my sweet lord," she managed to get out after some heavy panting. "I think I feel something down there," she told the nurse.

"I don't think so. This is your first baby, I'm pretty sure…"

The loudest grunt I have ever heard a human make came from my wife then as we all looked on in horror. "Get my panties off, the baby's gonna get stuck in them."

"Never want to hear those words in that sequence ever again," Deck chimed in as he turned to go to the waiting room, or another state, if he was smart.

I reached down and moved to take Anna's panties off and that's when I saw it. A head of brown hair was staring at me from between my woman's thighs and I don't mean her pussy hair that she hadn't been able to reach to trim either. "Holy fuck! There's a baby's head down here!" I shouted the words and everything stopped even though we were in the middle of the hallway with my wife sitting in a wheelchair. I moved my hands in front of her to catch our daughter just in case she fell out. "Can babies just fall out? Jesus fuck!"

"Oh my word!" The nurse declared as she started barking orders and then there was a rush of bodies all around us and I was being nudged out of the way as a doctor took my place.

The flurry of activity pushed me even further from Anna, but when her eyes popped open after the last push they met mine immediately, like she knew exactly where I was at all times. She gave me a quick smile and then pushed again. Her hair was plastered to her forehead with sweat and, before I could really take in the fact that her face changed immediately from pain-laced effort to tranquility, I heard it. A squall that shattered my heart to pieces and rebuilt it all at the same time. That was when I started pushing the staff out of the way. Hell, with the clusterfuck of people converged on my wife, there was no way to know who actually worked here and who didn't.

"Oh my goodness! Did my baby just deliver my first grandchild in the hallway?" Lucy and Double-D were running down the corridor to get to us as a woman snatched the baby from the doctor as he attempted to hand her over to Anna. I moved to block her exit immediately.

"Where the fuck do you think you're taking my baby?"

"We need to measure her and clean her up," she stated coolly.

"This is not a secure fucking hospital room we're standing in and I don't know you from Dick or Jane. That shit is not happening. You put the baby in wife's arms right this fuckin' minute and we'll worry about everything else when we get to a room."

"You can't tell me what to do, we have protocol," the woman stated as she tried to back away from me only to find Double-D standing at her back now keeping her from moving away.

"I will not tell you again," I seethed through clenched teeth.

"Carmen!" The doctor snapped in her direction. "Do as they say, and don't ever grab a baby that I am handing to its mother like that again or I will see that you no longer have a place here. Mr. Masters is not wrong." He turned his attention from the nurse in question once she handed the baby over to Anna, refusing to put her in my arms after she was scolded in front of her coworkers.

"Get her out of here. If I see that bitch at all again while my wife and daughter are here, I will sue this fucking hospital and that will feel like a slap on the wrist compared to what I do personally."

Everyone stopped briefly to glance at me and see how serious I was. Then the buzz of movement swept through the crowd once more. "Let's get them moved into a room, quickly. Anna still needs to deliver the rest," the doctor told them.

"The rest? There's another one in there?" I heard Double-D ask.

I saw, out of the corner of my eye, as Lucy popped his head with her hand as she giggled at him. "He's talking about the afterbirth dummy. You would know if you had stuck around after Anna was born."

"You told me to follow the baby," he argued back.

"You're darn right I did." She winked at me then. "Look, your son-in-law didn't have to be told to do that."

"What? Luce, that's not funny."

We were in the delivery suite and Anna was quickly transferred to a bed that had been broken down into one of the chairs that she sat in during her prenatal visits. The nurse helped her get her feet in the stirrups and the doctor went to town doing something down below that I quite frankly did not want to have nightmares about, so I didn't look.

What did catch my attention was the fact that Anna had popped a boob out, not caring who was looking, and our little girl was rooting around on her tit like she had been training for it all her life. When my baby girl latched onto my woman and started suckling from her, my heart leaped into my throat, choking me with emotion. I didn't even realize I was crying until Lucy leaned over and handed me a tissue. "That's a beautiful sight, isn't it?" She whispered to me.

"That is the best thing I have ever seen in my life," I told her.

**

EPILOGUE

ANNA

Dear Diary,

It's hard to believe that our daughter is four months old already. Tabby is an angel who was sleeping through most nights. The girl loves to eat and sleep, but she does not enjoy being messy at all. Evan thought it meant she was going to end up being super high maintenance when she was older. As a third generation MC Princess, I had no doubt that was true. She was already loved by more people in her short life than most people had in a lifetime.

Enough about that though, because I'm really writing to talk about our special day. My daughter and I both wore white gowns with peach flourishes through them. My gown was fitted through the bodice and the silky peach material underneath was topped with intricately designed lace swirls and flourishes. From a distance, it appeared the beautifully crafted lace portion of the dress was all that there was until it swept out loosely at the bottom. There, the lace fading into the silk slip of the dress where it trailed behind me as I walked. It didn't quite trail half-way down the church aisle like I once dreamed of, but it was stunning all the same. I didn't wear a veil, tiara, or any other adornment in my hair. It was curled and pinned back off my face to trail down behind my back. It was very similar to the style I had worn the first time I had been married.

Tabby was wearing an ivory dress with a pretty little peach satin ribbon tied around the waist into a big bow in the back. Her shoes matched the bow, as did the one holding up her little duck fluff tuft of chocolate brown hair on the top of her head. I leaned down to kiss my darling little girl and was rewarded with her giggles for my effort before my momma barged into the room we were getting ready in.

"Look at the two of you!" My momma breathed the words out as she took us in from head to toe. The shimmer of tears in her eyes couldn't be hidden as she spoke. "This is what…" My momma caught herself before as she saw my smile slip. I had forbidden anyone from mentioning the previous wedding at the courthouse. That disaster of a day took place exactly one year ago today. Instead of continuing on with whatever she'd been about to say, my momma changed her mind and added to my beautiful memories of the day. "This is what every bride dreams of looking like on her wedding day," my mother finally managed to get out. Even though she changed her wording I still got the gist of the meaning.

Everything about today is what last year was supposed to be like for me. It was what I had often dreamed of when I was growing up. I had even written about it my other diaries over the years. While my daughter and I might have looked fancy for this wedding it was not much more extravagant than the one we had in the courthouse. It was a simple affair in the little church just down the road from where my parents' house was located with only a few special guests in attendance. Once my momma had seen that we were settled and ready for our walk down the aisle, she opened the door to my father. He stood proudly in his tuxedo with arms out to hold my daughter. Once she was in his left arm, he crooked his right for me to place mine there so he could walk us to my husband who was waiting at the altar.

Merc, Tiger Lily, Deck, Ever, Kane, Gretchen, Beth, and J-Bird were the only people in attendance besides my parents. It was important to me that only the people who I had wanted to see our union happen. Crow and his old lady had been hurt that they hadn't been invited, but I couldn't see the man the same way I had growing up after hearing about the way he treated Ever all those years. The way he continued to treat her, as if she were a pariah, didn't sit right with me either. He could either love and have us all in his life, or none of us. At least, he wouldn't have me any longer. I readily admit I had my head stuck firmly in the sand for a long time. I was always so lost in my own worlds that I didn't notice the different way people treated my sister. I just assumed they felt the same about her as everyone did about me.

Part of growing up was learning that some of the things you thought were true as a child just aren't so. Today was all about that realization too. I always thought this was what my first wedding would have looked like. It didn't. Despite that, I was lucky, because this wedding was our do-over for the time when we were too young, too immature, too angry to get it right. We both failed one another in different ways in the beginning, and then we both also took a leap and hoped that things could be different. They have been different.

Tears began to mist my eyes as we started walking toward the man who I had pledged my heart to. The man who had given me the precious baby in my father's arms. The man who couldn't take his eyes off of me as I made slow progress getting to him while trying not to trip on the stupid long train. Why had

I ever thought that would be cool?

I saw the sheen of wetness in Evan's eyes too as we approached those final steps that would put me back in his arms. He too had worn a tux today with a peach Dahlia stuck into his lapel. His eyes met mine and I got lost in them as my father placed my hand in Evan's before leaning in to kiss my cheek, and taking my daughter to sit in the front pew with my momma.

We said our vows to one another with everyone watching as we placed rings on each other's fingers this time. I could also hear the snapping shutter of a camera as Beth, no doubt, caught the moments for us. Then the other missing piece from our previous wedding was upon us.

"You may kiss your bride." A fog had been lifted as the man spoke, because honestly I couldn't remember much before that besides staring into Evan's eyes. My husband didn't hesitate to take me fully into his arms, and with a smile that lit up his entire face, he brought his mouth down on mine in a searing kiss that took my breath away. As he pulled away he whispered, "I am yours. Always and only yours."

It was my turn to kiss my groom because there were no more perfect words than the ones he had just spoken. When we broke free of the kiss I returned his words to him, promising the same. "Always and only yours."

ACKNOWLEDGMENTS

My first acknowledgment goes to every one of you who will undoubtedly ask me "but what happened with this (enter information you want here)?" I promise, there are two more books in the series, and all of the loose ends will be tied up nice and tight by the end. Some you think are tied already might not be, so just hold on tight… I'm getting there!

The second acknowledgment is for the scene where Anna is giving birth to Tabby. I can already hear my critics shouting to the heavens about child birth never being like that. ☺ Well, this is one of those cases of art imitating life, because when my youngest daughter was born I kept telling the staff that I could feel her coming out and they didn't believe me. Then the man who was there to do my epidural (the first time I tried to get one of those too) told the nurse to humor me and look. Guess what? She was shocked by the head full of black hair she could see down there, and the doctor barely made it in the room to play catcher! Everyone has a different experience. I have four children, and they all left me with interesting child birth stories from early labor to late arrivals, and a kid who managed to get stuck because he had a giant head. ☺ It can, has, and does happen.

Now that my little anecdote is out of the way…

This book wasn't supposed to be finished until sometime in 2020. I say that, because I need to in order to acknowledge everyone here that deserves it. The Charleston Chapter of the Aces High MC World was not supposed to be written until LAST. I was saving it because I knew it was going to be a bit different from others of its genre. The problem with my "best laid plans" is always that my creativity rules me. Sometimes, that's an amazing thing. Other times, it is a burden that forces me to have to change those plans I had intentions of keeping. I plotted out what was originally about a 17-25 book world way back in 2016, with some of the ideas having been sitting around since 2014 just waiting for me to get the time to dive in. I had originally planned to release my MC world of books like this:

The S.H.E. Series first with the Aces High books coming in as a sort of spin-off world. ☺ As you know, things didn't happen that way at all. It was always supposed to be:

The S.H.E. Series with Angel Girl, Key, JoJo, Tash, and Legs (in that order) then three novellas (Evermore, MiMi, and Sweet Angel). Then I was going to release The Dakotas Series (which only had four books planned), Cedar Falls (with three books planned), Tallahassee (four books planned), Sierra High (three books planned) and then finally the Charleston Series (as a four book interconnected series).

As you all know, that is not at all how I moved into the publication process, because my muse took me off the path I'd designed. She's a bitch like that. That brings me back to how in the world the Charleston Series was the second to launch after the Dakotas.

I had nearly gone into writer retirement the prior year (2017) after releasing three books that didn't really do anything (Dancing with Danger, The Infinite Something, and one written under another name). Then I sat down at my computer in December 2018, and stumbled across my initial outline for The Other Princess. It wasn't the complete outline I had done on paper though. I searched everywhere and couldn't find the rest of the paper version so I started trying to remember what I had plotted out in order to fill in the blanks on the electronic outline. As I did, I got sucked into the world, ended up outlining book two as well, and then I wrote the entire first book in about two weeks. I figured, what the hell, I'll just throw it out into the world since it's finished and see what happens.

What happened blew my mind! That book broke a lot of personal records for me, but before that happened I went back to work (day job). Then I started writing Redemption Weather, because the characters were the next ones begging to be written. That meant I would literally have three first books in three different series in a world where none of them had been my initial starting point.

THE PRINCESS *and the* PROSPECT

Sticking to my plans when I haven't felt it before has led to crippling writer's block, so I tried something new this year. I just let my creative side do its thing. Now, here we are… my most prolific publication year since I started out in this novel writing business a decade ago. While publishing all these books, I have still managed to run into stumbling blocks. I've had chronic back issues which are made no better by the amount of time I'm sitting to get this work done. I've dealt with a computer crashing and losing a good deal of work I'd already had finished, and I've had other familial issues that popped up too. Life – she gives and takes so freely. That leads me to this moment, where I thank everyone who has had patience with me as I attempt to roll out close to TWENTY freaking books for 2019! I'm half way there with this book, and with less time than I'd like to get the other half done thanks to the stumbling blocks I spoke of!

I'd like to thank everyone who has stood by me while I worked, offered encouragement, sent in any editing issues you've found (and there are bound to be some considering the timetable I'm running on), and to those who have promoted my work. I appreciate every ounce of time you have put into my books. Whether it's just reading them for enjoyment and moving on, or taking the time to help promote – THANK YOU! Thank you again for your patience too. Things happen, and I am the queen of equalizing luck this year, it seems. In all seriousness for every bit of good luck I've had a setback that has kicked my ass. This year, I refuse to let that deter me though.

Now, I'd like to drop a major thank you to the following people who have been there, working hard behind the scenes, or who have just been super supportive of me this year.

First my children – who have had to fight for time with me this year thanks to the crazy schedule I'm keeping. I love you guys!

To my oldest daughter – Bella Hickman – who has come to work for me full time in order to help ease some of the burden of the afore mentioned brutal schedule. She has been instrumental in making sure I get most (I wish I could say all) of my books out on time this year. If not for her, I would have buried myself in the work and probably not been seen or heard from again. She also made our first public book signing a huge success with her vivacious personality since I was basically the author with a horrible case of resting bitch face who grimaced at everyone (my back was killing me – I'm a twat when I'm in pain). So – THANK YOU to Bella who rescued me this year.

To Barbara Gordon – who keeps me on my toes and is still bugging me about that book I was supposed to write eight years ago! I'm an asshole for not going back to finish that up yet, but she still hangs in there with me – hoping that one day I'll go back to it. In the meantime, she also points out things like book events I should definitely sign up for! So, if you see me at an event, chances are you should thank Barb for it. You should also thank her for the goodies I have to give away, because I've taken a lot of advice from her on what people love to pick up. I Can't thank you enough, Barb! You've been amazing through a lot of years. I'm looking forward to seeing you at Apollycon, 2020. For the rest of you reading that – I will be there as a reader, not a writer, but don't be shy if you see me there.

To one of my favorite people, and fellow author, John Abramowitz – who probably won't even know this is here because romance is not his genre – THANK YOU! When I was at my lowest point, you were there making sure I was okay and handling things. I can never repay you for being my person! The shoulder to whine on, the person to joke with, and the one to draw me into arguments (even though they're pointless when we both debate the same side) which drew me out of my shell and made me face the world on days I didn't want to face it anymore. Over the years, you have become my family. There are no take-backs. You're stuck with me now! Thank you for being there, and for being the first one to message me with congratulations when my books have taken off. You are a lovely cheerleader! Don't ever let anyone tell you otherwise! 😊

To Heather Brown – You have done so much in promoting my books, that I can't ever thank you enough! I appreciate every single minute you have worked on getting the word out. If you heard about my books, stumbled across some mention of them on social media, then you probably have Heather to thank.

Then there are all the other people, many of whom I have had the pleasure to meet this year. Linda, Jamie, Sarah, Josie, Rebecca, Belinda, Brianna, Rebel, Jo, Ang, and so many more… You have all done so much, and gone above and beyond to help promote books when you didn't have to. I appreciate you all so more than you know! Thank you.

JDRF DONATIONS

THANK YOU FOR YOUR DONATION!

This is a special thank you to my readers for purchasing this (and any other Aces High MC books). Ten percent of all royalties from the Aces High MC books and merchandise go to charity, Juvenile Diabetes Research Fund (JDRF) to be exact.

As many of you know, my youngest daughter, Lexy, is a Type 1 Diabetic. She was diagnosed in Dec. 2012, after nearly dying from going into DKA (diabetic ketoacidosis).

DKA is what happens when your body can't use the sugar in the body properly and ends up making acids with it instead. Those acids build up and will eventually kill the person if left untreated. We have struggled and fought every day since to make sure she has a normal life despite all the blood sugar checks and things she has to attach to her body (or all the shots she has to take) in order to survive. We've managed all this time to never have her get sick enough to require hospitalization or even a trip to the ER (for diabetic related issues).

I credit JDRF and Palmetto Children's Hospital in Columbia, SC (where she was diagnosed) for that. They gave us a diabetic bible to live by. We received a small backpack full of information that we still have, and use, to this day. It keeps us on track, and has given my daughter a better chance of not having complications later on in life from Diabetes.

Thank you for reading and for helping us to help make sure other families have access to that same information so that they can hopefully manage this horrible, life-long condition as well.

XOXO,
Christine & Lexy

ABOUT THE AUTHOR

Christine Michelle writes contemporary romance books from her fabulous home tucked away near the southern tip of the Appalachian Mountains on the North Carolina / Georgia border. That means she sees a lot of rainy days to help her focus, but when the sun comes out she's usually out and about playing in the woods, a creek, river, or lake.

She spends her free time with family, JoJo (her dog), and Simi (her cat who behaves more like a dog than the dog does).

Moonlit Dreams Publications website:

http://www.moonlitdreams.org

Goodreads (Christine M. Butler)

https://www.goodreads.com/author/show/354490.Christine_M_Butler

Goodreads (Christine Michelle):

https://www.goodreads.com/author/show/6035096.Christine_Michelle

Instagram:

https://www.instagram.com/christine_m_butler/

Facebook:

https://www.facebook.com/AuthorChristineMichelle